What was she doing in bed with Gabriel? What was she doing kissing her boss?

She hadn't actually kissed him, Tess told herself, grasping desperately at any straw that might somehow make the situation less than excruciatingly, appallingly, embarrassing.

"I'm sorry about that. I don't know what happened there," Gabriel said with effort.

"I don't know either," she said huskily. "One minute I was dreaming, and the next..." She trailed off as the memory flamed between them.

"I'd forgotten about what happened last night," Gabriel went on.

Clutching the duvet to her chest, Tess eyed him uneasily. "What *did* happen?" she asked.

"You invited me to share the bed."

From boardroom...to bride and groom!

A secret romance, a forbidden affair, a thrilling attraction?

Working side by side, nine to five—and beyond....
No matter how hard these couples try
to keep their relationships strictly professional,
romance is definitely on the agenda!

But will a date in the office diary
lead to an appointment at the altar?

Find out in this exciting new miniseries
from Harlequin Romance®.

Look out for
His Secretary's Secret (#3698)
by Barbara McMahon
on sale in April

Readers are invited to visit Jessica Hart's
Web site at www.jessicahart.co.uk

ASSIGNMENT: BABY
Jessica Hart

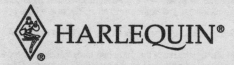

TORONTO • NEW YORK • LONDON
AMSTERDAM • PARIS • SYDNEY • HAMBURG
STOCKHOLM • ATHENS • TOKYO • MILAN • MADRID
PRAGUE • WARSAW • BUDAPEST • AUCKLAND

ISBN 0-373-03688-4

ASSIGNMENT: BABY

First North American Publication 2002.

Copyright © 2001 by Jessica Hart.

CHAPTER ONE

Fresh from her success in last Friday's award ceremony, Britain's favourite redhead, TV presenter Fionnula Jenkins, arrives at London's hottest restaurant, Cupiditas, with Gabriel Stearne, founder of US construction giant Contraxa (above). The couple met in New York, where Fionnula attended a charity ball sponsored by Contraxa. Entrepreneur Gabriel's activities are more usually reported in the financial pages, but since arriving in London he has been seen out several times with Fionnula, who refused to confirm speculation that he had moved to England to be with her. 'We just enjoy each other's company,' she said.

TESS had barely finished reading the caption when the door to the inner office opened, and she shoved the paper hurriedly out of sight in the wastepaper bin beneath her desk.

By the time Gabriel appeared, shrugging himself into an overcoat, she was innocently absorbed in typing up the letters he had dictated earlier.

'I'm going to a meeting with our insurers,' he said, brusquely buttoning his coat. 'Have those letters ready by the time I get back. I want a copy of the design report and the architects' files on my desk. All of them. In date order.'

'Yes, Mr Stearne,' said Tess.

Her voice was cool, with just a hint of a Scottish accent. Gabriel eyed her sardonically. She was watching him over the spectacles she wore when she was working, pen poised to note his instructions, the very model of a perfect PA.

In the four weeks she had worked for him he had learned

only three things about Tess Gordon. She was exception-
ally efficient. She was always immaculately groomed.

And she didn't like him one little bit.

Too bad, thought Gabriel indifferently. He wasn't here
to be liked. He was here to drag this company into the
twenty-first century and give himself the toe-hold he
needed into Europe, and worrying about what the icy Ms
Gordon thought about him was very low down his priority
list.

'When you've done that, you can send an e-mail reminding all staff that the phones are not for their personal
use,' he went on in a hard voice. 'That goes for e-mail as
well. A monitoring system is going to be introduced
shortly, so they'd better start getting used to it now.'

An order like that would no doubt cause a furore, but
Tess didn't react. She just made a note on her pad and
kept her inevitable reflections to herself.

'Any messages?' Gabriel asked curtly.

'Your brother rang. He asked if you could ring him
back.'

Gabriel grunted, and privately Tess marvelled that he
could be related to the irreverent American with the voice
like warm treacle who had rung while his brother was clos-
eted in his office. 'No calls,' Gabriel had said, and after a
month Tess knew better than to try and interrupt him, no
matter how important the caller might be.

Greg, as he had introduced himself, was evidently an
incorrigible flirt. Tess, braced to dislike anyone even remotely associated with Gabriel, had found him charming.
He had been warm, funny, sympathetic...everything his
brother was not!

Unaware—or, more likely, uncaring—of the unflattering
comparisons she had drawn, Gabriel was checking that he
had all the relevant papers for his meeting in his attaché
case. 'Anything else?'

'No,' said Tess, but she hesitated and Gabriel looked up

from the case. He had very light, very keen grey eyes that were a startling contrast to his strong, black brows, and she still hadn't got used to the way they seemed to look right through her.

'What?' he demanded.

'I wondered what time you would be back, that was all.'

'About six-thirty. Why?'

'I was hoping to have a word with you.' Tess's calm expression gave no hint of her inner trepidation.

Gabriel frowned. 'What about?'

Nobody could ever accuse him of beating about the bush, thought Tess with an inward sigh. She had to ask him for a rise, but it wasn't the kind of thing you could blurt out just like that.

'I'd rather explain when you're in less of a hurry,' she said.

'Can't it wait until tomorrow?'

'We'll be busy putting the Emery bid together tomorrow,' Tess pointed out. And then it would be the weekend, which would mean two more days to worry about Andrew. She set her teeth. It went against the grain to beg, but she had to try. 'If you could spare me five minutes when you get back, I would appreciate it.'

Gabriel looked at her. She had one of those faces that made it almost impossible to tell what she was thinking. It wasn't that she was unattractive. She had a fine-boned face with clear skin and beautiful eyebrows, and her hair, always pulled neatly back, was an unusual golden-brown colour. She might even be pretty, he thought dispassionately—if she ever lightened up and got rid of that snooty expression of hers.

It occurred to him suddenly that she might be going to hand in her notice, and his black brows drew together. He didn't have the time to find a new PA with this crucial contract coming up. He had inherited Tess when he'd taken over SpaceWorks, and her knowledge of the company was invaluable. He couldn't afford to lose her just yet. It was worth putting up with the frosty atmosphere until he got things under control.

'Very well,' he said, irritable at the thought of wasting precious time trying to cajole her into staying. 'If you wait until I get back, I'll see you then.'

'Thank you.'

That was typical Tess. No gush or fuss, just a cool thank you. Gabriel had never seen her anything but crisp, composed, competent. In many ways she was the ultimate personal assistant. She never flapped. When he shouted, she didn't get upset or muddled. She was intelligent and discreet. Gabriel knew that she was ideal.

It was just that he would like her more if she made the occasional mistake.

Or smiled.

Annoyed to realise that he'd allowed himself to be diverted, Gabriel shut his attaché case with snap and headed for the door. 'Oh, and book a table at Cupiditas,' he remembered at the last moment. 'Tonight, nine o'clock.'

Why could he never use the word 'please'? Tess wondered. It wasn't that hard to say. 'For two?'

'Yes, for two,' he barked, irritated anew by her composure. Most people either fawned or trembled in his presence, but not Tess. No, she just sat there in her sensible grey suit and looked down her nose at him.

'Certainly, Mr Stearne,' she said.

Gabriel scowled. 'I'll be back later,' he said, and strode out.

The moment he had gone, Tess retrieved the paper from the bin and smoothed out the crumpled page as she read the caption again, shaking her head in disbelief. Gabriel Stearne and Fionnula Jenkins! Who would have thought it?

All day, e-mails had been flying around the office about their unpopular new boss's appearance in the gossip columns. Tess had seen them, and had assumed that it was all some kind of joke until one of the other secretaries had brought along a copy of yesterday's paper to show her.

Now she studied the photograph, half expecting to spot that it was all a mistake, but no, it was definitely Gabriel. No one else had brows like that! Some of the girls in the office claimed to find him attractive, and were always dropping by in the hope of catching a glimpse of him, but Tess couldn't see what the fuss was about. To her, Gabriel wasn't broodingly handsome. He was just surly.

And there he was in the paper, looking as grimly formidable as ever, with Fionnula Jenkins clinging girlishly to his arm and smiling that famous Fionnula smile. Tess had never seen a more mismatched pair. Fionnula had all the gloss and glitz of a star. Gabriel was a workaholic, abrupt, impatient and, in Tess's opinion at least, downright rude.

What did a celebrity like Fionnula see in him? Tess wondered as she tossed the paper back in the bin and dialled the restaurant's number. Fionnula was beautiful and successful. She could have anybody she wanted, so why pick on Gabriel? It couldn't be money, as Fionnula had plenty of her own, and it certainly wasn't charm.

Perhaps, mused Tess, Fionnula was the kind of girl who liked a challenge. Gabriel's reputation had preceded him from the States. He was known to be utterly ruthless and unsentimental. If Fionnula thought she could find a heart beating somewhere beneath that steely exterior, good luck to her, thought Tess wryly. She was welcome to him.

By six, she had everything ready for Gabriel's return. His table was booked, and the letters, files and reports lay neatly arranged on his desk. Tess checked them automatically. She knew Gabriel was waiting to catch her out, but so far she hadn't made so much as a typing error for him to complain about. It had become an unacknowledged battle of wills between them and, in a perverse kind of way, Tess almost enjoyed the challenge of keeping up with the punishing pace he set.

Now, she squared up the last paper and mentally congratulated herself. Gabriel would have to try a bit harder if he wanted her to be unable to cope.

Back at her desk, she sent Andrew a quick e-mail to tell him a cheque was on its way, and that she hoped to be able to send him more next week, and was just rehearsing the arguments she would make to Gabriel for a rise when the phone rang.

'I've got a visitor here for Mr Stearne,' said the receptionist. 'She won't give her name, but she says it's personal.'

Tess looked at her watch. Gabriel hadn't said anything about a visitor. She hoped this didn't mean he wouldn't have time to listen to her request for a rise after all. 'You'd better send her up,' she said, suppressing a sigh.

She wasn't quite sure what she had expected Gabriel's visitor to be like, but it certainly wasn't the woman of about sixty who pushed a pram into the office a few minutes later.

Trying not to show her surprise, Tess took off her glasses and stood up with a polite smile. 'Can I help you?'

The woman looked around her as if she couldn't decide whether to be daunted or impressed. 'I'm looking for Gabriel Stearne,' she told Tess with a belligerent air.

'I'm afraid he's not here at the moment. I'm his assistant,' Tess explained. 'Perhaps I can help you?'

'I don't know if you can.' Digging around under the pram, the visitor pulled out a copy of yesterday evening's paper. It was folded open at the picture of Gabriel and Fionnula, and she tapped the photo. 'This *is* your Gabriel Stearne?' she asked doubtfully.

Tess looked down at the stern mouth, the dark, striking

brows and the unsmiling face next to the sparkling Fionnula. 'Yes, that's Mr Stearne,' she said.

'He's not what I expected,' the woman confessed, frowning down at the picture with Tess. 'Leanne said he was gorgeous. The most handsome man she'd ever met, she said.' Her mouth turned down disparagingly. 'I wouldn't call him handsome, myself, would you?'

'Not personally, no,' said Tess. It wasn't a very loyal answer, but it was hard enough putting up with his bad temper without having to rave about his looks as well.

'Ah, well, that's love for you.'

There was a tiny pause. 'Love?' she echoed cautiously.

'That's what Leanne called it. Leanne's my daughter,' the woman explained, seeing that Tess was still looking mystified. 'She met Gabriel on a cruise last year. She's a croupier,' she added proudly, 'and he was one of the first-class passengers. She said he was a lot of fun.'

A puzzled look came over her face as she looked around the plush office. 'Somehow I didn't imagine him somewhere like this. Leanne always said he was a free spirit.'

She wasn't the only one who was puzzled. Tess was still trying to come to terms with the idea of Gabriel hanging around in a casino and being a lot of fun, let alone a free spirit! She would love to know what the unknown Leanne was like.

'Well, I'm sorry he's not here,' she said after a moment. 'He won't be back until later. Can I give him a message?'

'You can do better than that,' said the woman, appearing to make up her mind abruptly. 'You can give him his son.'

For once Tess was shaken out of her composure. 'His *son*?' she repeated stupidly.

'That's right.' She nodded towards the pram. 'Harry, his name is.'

Tess stared at the pram as well. Gabriel, a father? It seemed very unlikely. 'Um…does he *know* about Harry?' she asked delicately.

'No.' The woman's mouth closed like a trap. 'Leanne would have it that he wasn't the kind of man you could tie down. I wanted her to tell him about Harry when he was born, but she wouldn't. She was determined to look after him herself. That's all very well, I said, but what about the money side of things? She was going to get a job at home, but then they offered her another contract on the ship. It was just for six weeks, and such good money that she couldn't turn it down.'

Tess was getting confused. She didn't quite understand what her unexpected visitor was trying to say, but one thing she was sure of: the last thing Gabriel would want was to come back to the office and find himself presented with a baby. She would have to stick to essentials.

'I think it's up to your daughter to discuss any paternity issues with him,' she said firmly. 'Mr Stearne keeps his private life quite separate from the office.'

'Leanne's not here to discuss anything,' the woman pointed out. 'That's just the point. The thing is,' she confided, 'I said I'd look after Harry for her while she was away, but a few days ago I heard that I'd won a trip to California. Me! It's the first time I've won anything!

'I've always wanted to go to the States,' she went on wistfully, 'but it means flying out straight away, and I thought I was going to have to turn it down until I saw in the paper last night that Gabriel Stearne was over here. I don't see why I should give up my holiday when Harry's father can look after him just as well.'

'I don't know about that,' said Tess, alarmed. 'He's extremely busy.'

'Not so busy he can't swank around with that Fionnula Jenkins,' said Harry's grandmother, brandishing the paper as proof. 'If he's got time to do that, I reckon he's got time to look after his own son. If you ask me, it's high time he took some responsibility for him. Why should

Leanne have to cope all by herself? She didn't get pregnant by herself, did she?'

'Well, no, obviously not, but—'

'It's not as if I'm leaving him for ever. I'm only going for a fortnight. He's a good baby—he won't be any trouble.'

Tess came hurriedly round the desk as she realised just what the other woman was saying. 'You're not seriously thinking of leaving the baby here?' she said, appalled.

'Why not? From everything Leanne ever said, your precious Gabriel isn't short of a bob or two. I'm sure he'll manage.'

'But you can't just abandon him!'

The woman's chin set stubbornly. 'I'm not abandoning him. I'm leaving him with his father.' She leant over the pram and kissed the baby. 'You be a good boy, love. Your gran'll be back for you in a couple of weeks.'

She glanced at Tess and pointed at the rack underneath the pram. 'He's got everything he needs for a couple of days, but you'll need to buy some more formula and nappies after that.'

'*Nappies?*' Tess was aghast. 'You can't just *go*,' she cried, but the baby's grandmother was already heading for the lifts. 'Look, wait!' she called, hurrying after her. 'Wait!'

But her cry had woken the baby, who promptly began to yell. Distracted, Tess hesitated in the doorway. She couldn't believe his grandmother wouldn't come back to the crying child, but when she ran out into the corridor she was in time to see the lift doors closing and the other woman had gone.

Frantically, Tess pressed the button to call the lift back, only to see its lights descending inexorably. She looked around for help, but the entire floor seemed to be deserted. Everyone else had obviously gone home at five-thirty, like sensible people. Tess wished fervently that she had done the same.

Behind her, Harry had redoubled his cries, and she took her finger off the button. There was no way she was going to catch his grandmother. By the time the lift came back she would be long gone.

Now what was she going to do?

In the office, she could hear the baby at full throttle. Hurrying back, she was alarmed to see that his face was red and contorted. What if he was having some kind of fit? She joggled the pram ineffectually for a while and, when that didn't work, picked him up and cuddled him gingerly against her shoulder the way she had seen her friend, Bella, do with her new baby.

'Shh, it's all right,' she told him, wishing that she believed it herself. Wryly, she remembered the smug way she had laid out the papers on Gabriel's desk and congratulated herself on being able to cope with whatever he threw at her! Her famous unflappability didn't extend to babies, which she found alarming at the best of times.

Tess threw a harassed look at the clock on the wall. If only Gabriel would come back!

It felt like two hours, but according to the clock it was only twenty minutes before Gabriel appeared. He walked into the office to be greeted by an unmistakable sigh of relief.

'Thank God you're back!' said Tess, who would have scorned the very idea of being pleased to see him when he had left only a matter of hours ago.

Gabriel stopped dead at the sight of her. He had left an icily efficient, immaculately groomed PA. He returned to find her clutching a snivelling baby, her pristine blouse crumpled by tears and tiny, clutching hands, and the honey-coloured hair escaping in wisps from its usually demure style.

The black brows contracted. 'What's going on?'

He might enjoy the sight of Tess less than her normal, coolly composed self, but the meeting with the insurers hadn't gone well. There was a good deal of work to be done to get the bid ready for the next day, and the very last thing he needed right now was a bawling infant cluttering up the office.

Gabriel eyed it askance. 'Whose is that baby?' he demanded, without even giving her a chance to reply to his first question.

By this stage Tess was too harassed to think of a way to break the news diplomatically. 'It's yours.'

'What?' he roared so loudly that Harry flinched and began to cry again.

'Don't shout! Now look what you've done!' she accused him. 'I'd just got him to stop, too.' She joggled the baby in her arms until his sobs subsided. 'There, that's better,' she murmured. 'The nasty man's not going to shout any more.'

Gabriel controlled his temper with an effort. 'Tess, will you please explain to me what you are doing with that baby?' he said ominously, laying his attaché case on her desk.

Over the sound of Harry's snuffling cries, Tess told him what she could remember. 'But it all happened so quickly,' she finished. 'One minute I was putting the letters on your desk, the next I was left holding the baby!'

'Let me get this right,' said Gabriel, a muscle beating dangerously in his jaw. 'A woman turns up out of the blue, tells you she's going on holiday and deposits a baby with you...and you let her walk away without even finding out her name?'

When he put it like that, it didn't sound as if she had handled the situation very well, Tess had to admit. 'She said you were Harry's father,' she said lamely.

'And you believed her?'

'I didn't know *what* to believe,' she said, forced onto

the defensive. 'You haven't exactly been forthcoming about your private life. For all I know, you've got a dozen sons!'

Gabriel glared at her. 'I can assure you,' he said in glacial tones, 'that I not only have no son, I've never even *been* on a cruise, and I certainly haven't seduced any stray croupiers without being aware of it.'

Biting her lip, Tess looked worriedly down at the baby in her arms. 'What are we going to do?' she asked.

'*We?*' He lifted his brows in a way that made her long to haul out and hit him.

'It's not my baby,' she pointed out tightly.

'It's not mine either,' he retorted, ignoring the danger signals snapping in Tess's brown eyes. 'You're the one who took responsibility for him. You deal with it.'

The dismissive note in his voice caught Tess on the raw. For a moment, she could only gape at him, torn between astonishment at the colossal nerve of the man and inarticulate fury at his callous lack of support.

'Now, just a minute—' she began furiously, but before she could tell Gabriel exactly what she thought of him, the phone on her desk began to ring, a loud, jarring sound that ripped through the tense atmosphere in the office. Involuntarily, they both turned to look at it.

Gabriel cursed under his breath at the interruption. 'You'd better answer it,' he said snidely. 'It might be someone else who wants a place to dump a child or a dog while they go on holiday! Why not tell them all to come along? Tell them we'll take care of their pot plants too!'

Tess glared at his sarcasm. 'How do you suggest I answer it?' she said through her teeth. 'In case it's escaped your notice, I've only got two hands and both are full at the moment! Or am I expected to pick up the phone with my teeth?'

The phone continued to ring insistently, impossible to ignore. 'Oh, all right, *I'll* get it,' snapped Gabriel.

He leant over the desk and picked up the phone. 'Yes?' he snarled. 'Oh…Greg…yes, I did get your message…no, there's nothing you can do,' he said brusquely, adding as an afterthought, 'unless you happen to know where I can find a croupier called Leanne?'

Tess couldn't hear what Greg was saying, but it was obviously not what Gabriel was expecting. She saw his face change, and he shot her a quick glance. 'Hold on a second,' he interrupted his brother, 'I think I'd better call you back. Give me two minutes.'

'That was my brother,' he said unnecessarily as he put down the phone. For once he seemed at a loss.

'Your brother? What's *he* got to do with Harry's mother?' asked Tess, bewildered by the unexpected turn of events.

'That's what I'm going to find out.' Gabriel sounded terse. Shrugging off his coat, he headed for his office.

There was something going on, thought Tess, aggrieved, and he clearly had no intention of telling her what it was! 'What am I supposed to do in the meantime?' she said crossly.

'Just…' he gestured vaguely '…keep the baby quiet.'

'Great, thanks a lot!' she muttered as the door shut firmly behind him.

She shifted Harry onto her other arm. He might be small, but he was surprisingly heavy, and she flexed the arm that had been supporting him with a grimace. He was grizzling into her neck, small, sniffling little sobs as if he wanted to cry but was too tired to make the effort.

Tess knew just how he felt. She looked at the clock again, and was amazed to find that it was less than an hour since she had looked up to see the pram being pushed into the office.

Not knowing what else to do with him, Tess walked around the office, patting Harry awkwardly on the back, the way she had seen her friends do with their babies. She wished Gabriel would hurry up. It was all very well for him to tell her to keep Harry quiet, but she couldn't walk up and down like this all night.

The sound of the door opening made her swing round, and Gabriel emerged in his shirt sleeves, looking grimmer than ever.

'Well?' she demanded.

Gabriel loosened his tie as if it felt too tight. 'Greg was on a Caribbean cruise last year,' he told her after a moment. 'He told me that he met a croupier called Leanne, and they had an affair while he was on the ship but, typically of Greg, he can't remember her surname, so we can't track down her mother that way. That doesn't mean that Greg is Harry's father,' he added quickly, 'but at least we know why your visitor picked on me.'

'She definitely said *Gabriel* Stearne,' objected Tess. 'It's not that easy to muddle up Gabriel and Greg.'

The suspicion in her voice made Gabriel grit his teeth. 'Look, you wanted to know what the situation was, and I'm telling you,' he said tautly. He didn't really want to tell Tess about Greg, and give her yet another reason to look down her snooty little nose at him, but she was obviously going to go on asking questions until she had some satisfactory answers. Briefly, Gabriel let himself think longingly of Janette, his PA back in the States, who accepted everything he said unquestioningly.

But Janette wasn't here, and Tess was.

'It turns out that Greg sometimes uses my name when it suits him to let people believe that the G in his name stands for Gabriel and not Gregory,' he told her, resigned. 'He says it gets him better tables in restaurants and seats on overbooked planes and, in the case of the cruise, he upgraded his cabin on the strength of my reputation. Having booked as Gabriel Stearne, he carried on using my name, and it was too late to change it when he met Leanne. Anyway, Greg didn't think it would matter. He knew I would never go on a cruise and it was very unlikely that Leanne would ever read the business pages and see my picture.'

'So it might not just be Leanne who thinks that she has had an affair with you? There could be girls all round the world who believe that you're incredibly handsome, a fantastic lover and great fun to be with?'

Gabriel shot Tess a suspicious look. Her face was quite straight, but there was glint in her eyes and a distinct undercurrent of sarcasm in her voice. Why didn't she come right out and say that the idea of anyone associating him with fun or believing him to be a wonderful lover was absolutely hilarious?

He scowled. 'Right now, we're only concerned with Leanne,' he said quellingly. Not that Tess seemed very quelled.

'And Leanne thinks that Greg is Harry's father?'

'Yes.'

'That would make Harry your nephew,' she said slowly, looking from one to the other as if looking for a resemblance.

'It's a possibility,' Gabriel admitted grudgingly, evidently less than thrilled at the prospect of a new addition to the family.

'Did Greg think that he might be Harry's father?'

Gabriel sat on the edge of her desk and rubbed the back of his neck a little wearily. 'I didn't tell him about Harry,' he said after a moment.

Tess was taken aback. Surely that had been the point of ringing Greg? 'Why not?'

'Because for once in his life, Greg is where he ought to be,' said Gabriel flatly. 'He's in Florida, with my mother. His father—my stepfather—is having open-heart surgery and my mother can't cope on her own. She's not strong at the best of times, and I'd rather he stayed and supported her than came haring over here. It's not as if he knows anything about babies.'

'Oh, unlike us?' said Tess, not even bothering to hide her sarcasm this time.

Gabriel ignored her. Straightening from the desk, he began to pace around the office. 'This is the last thing we need tonight,' he said, muttering under his breath. 'All the figures in our proposal are going to have to be checked, and I want to rewrite the section on our design policy. I haven't got time to run around London looking for an unnamed grandmother who's just dumped a baby here.'

'Why don't you ring the police?'

'I can't risk the story getting into the papers. If Greg does turn out to be the father, and my mother got to hear of it, she'd be devastated. She dotes on Greg and she's got enough to deal with at the moment with Ray so ill.'

Tess's arm was aching and she decided to try putting Harry back in his pram. How odd, she thought, as she rocked the pram tentatively, terrified that the baby would start crying again. She wouldn't have had Gabriel Stearne down as a devoted son, but he seemed to be making a lot of effort to spare his mother any trouble. Perhaps deep down he was human, after all? He certainly did a good job of hiding it most of the time!

Oblivious to her thoughts, Gabriel was contemplating his options. Thrusting his hands into his pockets, he hunched his shoulders and continued his pacing, up and down, up and down, until Tess longed to stick out a foot and trip him up.

'I could hire private investigators to track down the baby's mother,' he decided after a little while, frowning at the floor. 'There can't be that many croupiers called Leanne. Make a note to get onto them first thing tomorrow morning,' he added in an aside.

Tess refrained from leaping for her notebook. 'Even if they can find Leanne, she's still got to get back to this country,' she pointed out unhelpfully. 'What are you going to do with him until then?'

'That's what nannies are for.' Having made up his mind what needed to be done, Gabriel was already moving onto thinking about the proposal they had to submit the next day. His shoulders straightened. 'You'd better get hold of an agency now. Say I'll need a nanny for a week initially. With any luck, we'll have been able to track down his mother by then.'

Ready to dismiss the matter from his mind, he turned back towards his office. Tess looked at him in disbelief. 'It's almost seven o'clock,' she said, speaking very slowly and clearly so that he would be sure to understand. 'All the agencies will be closed. I won't be able to contact anyone until tomorrow morning at the earliest.'

Exasperated, Gabriel glowered at her, his jaw working in frustration. Logically, he knew that it wasn't Tess's fault, but her objections seemed designed to prevent him from getting on with more important things. He simply didn't have the time to deal with all this.

'What do you suggest, in that case?' he asked her through gritted teeth.

Tess smiled sweetly at him. 'You'll have to look after him yourself.'

'*Me?*'

'Yes, *you!*' she said, savouring the expression on his face. He looked so aghast that she nearly laughed. 'It seems that Harry is your responsibility, after all.'

'But I don't know one end of a baby from another!'

'It's only for a night,' she told him briskly. 'I'm sure it's just a matter of common sense.'

Gabriel eyed her with acute dislike. A matter of common sense, was it? *She* hadn't looked quite so confident when she'd been holding the baby, had she? He set his jaw.

'I can't do it on my own,' he said. 'You'll have to help me.'

'Sorry,' said Tess, not sounding the slightest bit apologetic. 'I'm going out tonight.'

'On a date?'

He stared at her with unflattering surprise. It had obviously never occurred to him before that she might actually have a life outside the office, let alone be attractive enough to have a date.

'Yes, a date,' she said, peeved, although it wasn't strictly true. She was only meeting some friends, but she didn't feel like telling him that. She was tired of being treated like a cardboard cut-out who got propped in the corner of the office every night!

'Couldn't you break it?'

Silently, Gabriel cursed his absent brother. It went against the grain to beg a favour from anyone, let alone from Tess Gordon with her frosty Scottish voice and her disapproving expression, but he was desperate. There was no way he was going to be left alone with that baby.

'Look, I know it's a lot to ask,' he went on, forcing the words out, 'but I need help. I can't manage Harry on my own. I've never even *held* a baby before.'

The edge of desperation in his voice couldn't help but strike a chord with Tess, but she hardened her heart, remembering how quick he had been to disclaim any responsibility for Harry at first. He hadn't exactly been supportive then, had he?

'You must have friends who could help you,' she said.

'I don't know anyone else in London,' said Gabriel. 'I've only been here a month.'

'Oh?' Tess thought of the newspaper in the bin under her desk. 'I did hear somewhere that you knew Fionnula Jenkins,' she said pointedly.

'Not well enough to ask her to give up her evening and a whole night to take care of a strange baby.'

'You don't know *me* very well, but you're asking me to do it.'

'That's different.' Gabriel glowered at her lack of logic. 'You work for me.'

'I'm your personal assistant, not a nanny!'

'Yes, and it would assist me personally if you helped me look after this baby tonight.'

Tess put up her chin. She wasn't going to be bullied into this! 'I'm sorry,' she said firmly, 'but I—'

'I'll pay you overtime, of course,' Gabriel interrupted her, switching tactics. 'Double the usual rate,' he added cunningly.

It was a masterly stroke. Fatally, Tess hesitated. She had been wondering how she was going to find the money to help Andrew out of his difficulties, and now here was an opportunity to earn some extra cash, without the need to grovel to Gabriel for a pay rise that he would almost certainly refuse.

Could she really afford to turn it down?

'I don't know any more about babies than you do,' she said, but Gabriel could tell she was weakening and he pressed home his advantage.

'You can't know less,' he said. 'Come on, Tess, you can't leave me on my own with him.'

When she thought about how prepared he had been to leave her on her own with Harry, Tess longed to be able to tell him that she most certainly could, but then she made the mistake of looking down at the baby. His face was puckering with misery, and she bent instinctively to pick him up. The poor wee mite had already been abandoned once today. She couldn't walk away and abandon him again.

CHAPTER TWO

SHE sighed. 'All right,' she said, 'I'll help you—but *help* is the operative word.' Lifting her chin, she met Gabriel's gaze with a challenging expression in her clear brown eyes. 'I'm not looking after him all by myself. You're going to have to do your share.'

'Fair enough,' said Gabriel, too relieved to object to any conditions. Anything was better than being left on his own with the baby. 'We'll take him to my apartment,' he went on quickly, before she had a chance to change her mind. 'I can drive you home to get whatever you need for the night, and then we can go straight on.'

He was all set to hustle her off there and then, but things were happening a bit too quickly for Tess's liking. 'We could do with some advice first,' she prevaricated, not sure she was ready to be swept off to Gabriel's apartment just yet. She might have agreed to help him, but there seemed to be a lot of things they hadn't discussed yet, and she wanted to be clear just what it was she had agreed to do.

'I thought you said all the agencies would be closed?' said Gabriel, frowning.

'I'm not talking about ringing an agency. I've got a friend who had a baby earlier this year. Since neither of us know what we're doing, I think it would be worth giving her a ring—if that's OK with you, of course,' she couldn't resist adding with an innocent look that didn't fool Gabriel for a moment. 'I know you don't like us making personal phone calls,' she reminded him virtuously.

'Yes, yes, get on with it!' snapped Gabriel, thinking that staff phone calls were the least of his problems right now.

To his horror, he found the baby thrust into his arms as

24

Tess reached across the desk to twist the phone round to face her. She had Bella's number on the phone's memory, but since she had just reminded Gabriel about his threatened crack-down on personal calls, she decided it would be wiser not to draw attention to it. That meant looking it up in her diary, which was something she rarely had to do with all the technology at her fingertips, and laboriously dialling the number in full.

Not that Gabriel was likely to have noticed. He had followed her to the desk, clearly in case he had to hand Harry quickly back, and was holding him awkwardly at arm's length, eyeing him with a mixture of trepidation and appalled fascination. Tess wouldn't have believed that anyone could look more uncomfortable with a baby than her, but Gabriel managed it easily.

The ruthless arrogance had been wiped from his face now he'd been presented with a baby, she noticed with some amusement. In his shirt sleeves, with his tie askew where he had been tugging at it in frustration, he seemed younger and much more approachable all of a sudden.

That had to be an illusion, thought Tess sourly. She had never met anyone *less* approachable than Gabriel Stearne. He was cold, unscrupulous, and completely out of touch with the people who worked for him, whom he treated with a blend of indifference and contempt.

And this was the man she was going to spend the evening with, she reminded herself with a sinking heart.

Oh, well, she thought, she would just have to keep thinking of the money.

Perching on the front of her desk, she listened to the busy beeping in her ear as the phone connected and watched Gabriel jiggle the baby nervously up and down. For a moment, Harry looked unsure whether he liked it or not and, as his face screwed up, Tess held her breath, waiting for the outraged wail that she was sure would follow.

But Harry didn't cry. He dissolved without warning into

a gummy and quite irresistible smile which left Gabriel completely nonplussed. Tess saw astonishment, relief and perplexity chasing themselves across his face, swiftly succeeded by a kind of baffled pride at the baby's unexpected reaction to his handling, before he smiled instinctively back at Harry.

Tess nearly fell off the desk. It was like running up to someone you thought you knew and finding yourself face to face with a perfect stranger. She had never seen Gabriel smile before—she had never even *imagined* him smiling—and she was caught off guard by the way the cold eyes lit with humour and the stern mouth relaxed, creasing his cheeks and revealing teeth that were strong and very white against his dark features.

Her heart jerked suddenly in her chest. If Gabriel had been taken aback by Harry's smile, it was nothing to her own reaction to his, and she hoped her own expression wasn't as easy to read. She felt jarred and breathless, and it was some moments before she realised that a puzzled voice was speaking in her ear.

'Hello...? Hello? Who is this?'

'Bella!' Tess jerked her gaze away from Gabriel and recollected herself with an effort. 'It's Tess.'

'Tess!' cried Bella in carrying tones. 'I haven't heard from you for ages! How's the boss from hell?'

'Standing right beside me,' said Tess thinly. She didn't dare look at Gabriel. Had he heard Bella or not?

As succinctly as she could, she explained the situation to her friend, but it wasn't easy with Bella exclaiming and interposing irrelevant questions, and it took Tess some time to get her to the point. Once, she risked a glance at Gabriel, who raised a sardonic eyebrow. He had heard all right.

'Just tell us what to do, Bella,' she said hastily. 'Harry's grandmother said that we would have everything we needed under the pram, but I might as well be looking under the bonnet of a car. There's a whole lot of stuff there, but I've got no idea how any of it works.'

Responding to her frantic gesture, Gabriel pushed the pram nearer, so Tess could describe the various packets and bits of equipment that had been packed onto the lower rack.

'Hmm.' Bella considered. 'How old is this baby?'

Tess covered the receiver with her hand, although since Gabriel had clearly already heard both sides of the conversation it seemed a little late for discretion. 'How old is Harry?' she asked him.

'How do I know?' he replied unhelpfully.

The 'boss from hell' jibe was still rankling, and he was annoyed to find that he had been distracted by the way Tess was leaning against her desk. She was wearing the same discreetly elegant grey suit she always wore, the same sensible court shoes, but she looked somehow different. Had she always had legs like that? Gabriel wondered. And, if so, how was it that he had never noticed them before?

'A baby is a baby, isn't it?' he added crossly, hoping that Tess hadn't noticed him staring.

'Apparently not,' she said, holding onto her own temper with an effort. It wasn't easy to concentrate on what Bella was saying when she could feel him frowning at her. Obviously Bella's comment hadn't gone down well.

Tough. Tess tried to convince herself that she didn't care. It wouldn't do Gabriel any harm to realise what they all thought of him, although the timing was less than ideal, she had to admit. If he had to learn how much she disliked him, it might have been better if it hadn't been *just* before they had to spend the entire night together!

Pushing the prospect to the back of her mind, Tess turned back to the problem of Harry's age. 'Did your brother mention when he was on this famous cruise?' she tried again.

'Some time last summer… August, I think he said.' Gabriel calculated quickly. 'That would make Harry about five months now.'

Tess, still trying to add nine months onto August, abandoned her attempts at mental arithmetic and uncovered the receiver once more. 'Five months, we think,' she told Bella.

'Hmm… And where exactly are you proposing to take this baby?'

'To Mr Stearne's apartment.'

'Oh?' Bella managed to invest two letters with at least sixteen syllables. 'You mean you're going to spend the *night* with him?'

Tess hadn't wanted to think about that aspect of the situation. Of course, she and Gabriel weren't going to be spending the night together in the way Bella meant, but still, there was something uncomfortably intimate about the thought of being alone with him in his flat.

Involuntarily, she glanced at Gabriel, who had heard both the words and the intonation. He didn't say anything, but he didn't need to. The faint lift of his brows spoke volumes. A man who went out with the likes of Fionnula Jenkins was hardly likely to have any problems keeping his hands off *her*.

Suddenly acutely aware of the wet patch on her blouse where Harry had pressed his face miserably into her shoulder, and of the wisps of hair escaping around her face, Tess turned her back on him and told Bella crisply not to be silly. 'It's simply a matter of looking after the baby until we can get hold of a nanny tomorrow. If you could just explain what we give him to eat, Bella…'

It took some time, but eventually Tess managed to extract instructions about sterilising bottles, heating milk, washing, winding and sleeping positions, all of which she scribbled down frantically, wishing that Bella wouldn't be quite so vague about exactly what to do and when.

When Bella had finished, Tess cast an eye over her notes and discovered that there was one thing missing.

'What about changing his nappy?' she asked at last, bracing herself.

'What about it?'

'Well, you know...how do we know when to do it?'

Bella laughed. 'Have you tried smelling him?'

Without being told, Gabriel lifted Harry nearer and sniffed cautiously. He wrinkled his nose and the downward turn of his mouth told Tess all she needed to know.

'Ah,' she said, her heart sinking. 'It looks as if we might have to tackle that now. What should we do?'

'Tess, I cannot believe that you've got to thirty-four without changing a nappy!' Bella scolded. 'If you took a more hands-on interest in your goddaughter, you'd know all this by now. And what's all this ''we'' business?' she went on before Tess had a chance to object. 'Since when did you get quite so cosy with Gabriel Stearne?'

Tess avoided looking at Gabriel, although she could feel him listening. *'Bella,'* she said through gritted teeth, 'could we just stick to the nappy changing?'

'Oh, all right, but you'd better ring me tomorrow and tell me *everything*!'

Noting down Bella's sarcastically simplistic instructions, Tess had the feeling she wasn't going to enjoy the next few minutes very much. 'Thanks, Bella,' she said dryly. 'I can't wait.'

'Good luck,' said Bella, and then raised her voice wickedly to make sure that Gabriel would hear her. 'And tell that boss of yours that I've always thought he sounded very sexy, whatever you say!'

Tess put the phone down hastily. She would kill Bella next time she saw her! Faint colour tinged her cheeks as she pretended to read over the instructions that Bella had given her.

What exactly *did* she say? Gabriel wondered darkly. Nothing very flattering, that was for sure!

'I didn't realise that you were in the habit of discussing me with your friends,' he said with a cold look.

'I didn't realise that *you* were in the habit of listening in to private conversations!' Tess snapped back, provoked, and they glared at each other.

Tired of being dangled from outstretched arms, Harry had begun to grizzle. Remembering just in time that he needed Tess's help that evening, Gabriel swallowed the savage retort on the tip of his tongue with an effort.

'Look, let's get this nappy changing over and done with,' he growled. 'We'll do it together, since it's obviously not going to be a very pleasant job.'

'All right.' Tess took the opportunity to back down too. The presence of Harry seemed to have a dangerously disinhibiting effect on both of them, and if she wasn't careful she would find herself out of a job altogether.

The extra money she would earn on overtime tonight might be useful, but her salary was essential, Tess reminded herself guiltily. She had been looking for another job ever since Gabriel had arrived at SpaceWorks, but all those she could have applied for would have meant taking a drop in salary that she simply couldn't afford at the moment. Standing up to Gabriel was one thing, provoking him into sacking her was another. It might be an idea to keep her mouth shut and keep her job, she reflected ruefully.

Still holding Harry at arm's length, Gabriel carried him through to the sleekly modern bathroom that was attached to his private office. There, after some discussion, they spread out a towel on the black marble surface by the basin and laid Harry on top of it.

'Well, here goes!' Tess took a deep breath and resolutely unbuttoned Harry's little body suit.

By now, Harry was crying in earnest and wriggling

alarmingly, and it took two of them to stop him squirming off the marble onto the floor while they worked out how to unfasten the nappy.

Both grimaced when it finally fell apart, and they looked at each other for a pregnant moment. Gabriel found himself staring into Tess's eyes and noticing with an odd, detached part of his mind that they were a beautiful shade of brown, the colour of clear honey, shot through with gold. He had never really seen her eyes before, he realised. Usually they were hidden behind the spectacles she wore when she was working at the computer or taking dictation, and looking into them now for the first time he felt as if he had received a tiny electric shock.

It was an odd feeling. Even odder was the strange tightening of the air between them as they looked at each other. Afterwards, Gabriel would think it could only have lasted a second or two, but at the time it seemed as if their eyes held for an eternity, and when Tess turned back to the protesting baby he felt unaccountably jarred, even dislocated.

Brushing the sensation from his mind, Gabriel set his jaw and forced his attention back to the messy business of changing Harry's nappy.

To Tess, it all seemed unbelievably complicated. She couldn't understand how the mothers she had seen deftly changing babies in washrooms managed on their own. She and Gabriel had to keep stopping to refer to Bella's instructions, and running backwards and forwards to the pram to find the various wipes and creams and spare nappies that seemed to be required.

Although she would have died rather than admit it, Tess was glad that Gabriel was there. It was a relief to discover that he was even more squeamish than she was, and by the time they had finished he was looking positively green about the gills, but his hands were very steady as he held Harry still. There was something oddly reassuring about them, Tess thought inconsequentially. They were big and square and competent, with very clean nails, and for some reason she was very conscious whenever her fingers brushed against his.

At last it was over. Harry, buttoned up again, was obviously more comfortable, and he stopped grizzling when Tess picked him up and cuddled him carefully against her shoulder. She must be getting the hang of it, she congratulated herself.

'Thank God that's over!' said Gabriel, disposing of the dirty nappy with distaste, and Tess found herself nodding in sympathy as their eyes met again. There was that same puzzling charge to the air, the same sense that a smile was lurking, waiting for the slightest excuse to shimmer between them, before Tess looked quickly away, more disturbed than she wanted to admit. It wouldn't do to start thinking that she and Gabriel had anything in common, even if it was only a squeamishness about nappies!

Fortunately, that uncomfortable sense of complicity didn't survive the trip down to the underground car park to Gabriel's car. Tess had frequently wondered why it took so *long* for friends with babies to do anything, but that evening she discovered that with a baby in tow you couldn't simply put on your coat, pick up your bag and go.

Harry refused to be put down in his pram, so they had to take it in turns to hold him while they repacked all his stuff, switched off lights and computers, and gathered up their own things. It all took forever, and then they had to negotiate the lift with the pram. They were halfway down before Gabriel remembered the papers he needed to check that night, so they had to go back up again.

His temper was not improved when they got to the car at last and had to work out how to collapse the pram. Cursing fluently under his breath, Gabriel wrestled with knobs and levers.

'It can't be that difficult,' said Tess unwisely. 'You see mothers with these prams the whole time. They can't all have degrees in mechanical engineering.'

'No, and they don't all have people hanging around making pointless remarks, either!' Gabriel snarled, and Tess bridled.

'There's no need to bite my head off just because you can't do it,' she said coldly, forgetting her earlier resolution to keep her tongue between her teeth. 'It's not my fault you're in a bad mood.'

Gabriel thought that was a matter of opinion. If she had dealt properly with Harry's grandmother, the evening wouldn't have turned into the unmitigated disaster it was already shaping up to be. As it was, he had been forced to beg for her help, had endured a revolting session with the baby's nappy, and was now making an idiot of himself struggling with this cursed pram.

And all he had to look forward to was an evening spent in the company of his PA, who had made no secret of the fact that she disliked him intensely. Gabriel reckoned that Tess had plenty to do with his bad mood, but he had to content himself with casting her a filthy look as he turned back to the pram. He vented his temper instead on a lever that he had already tried more than once, jerking it savagely towards him, and the pram collapsed in one smooth motion that smacked uncannily of reproach for his excessive use of brute force.

At last they were on the way, but almost immediately found themselves in heavy traffic heading south of the river to where Tess lived. Gabriel drummed his fingers impatiently on the steering wheel as they edged forward, annoyed to find himself very aware of Tess sitting beside him.

He wished he hadn't noticed her eyes. He wished he hadn't noticed her legs. He wished he hadn't noticed *any-*

thing different about her, because now that he had started noticing, it was somehow difficult to stop.

There was no reason to notice her. She hadn't done anything to attract him—quite the opposite, in fact—but Gabriel couldn't stop his gaze sliding sideways to where she sat staring haughtily out of the window. That exasperatingly crisp competence had deserted her for once, he noted with a kind of perverse satisfaction. If nothing else, this evening so far had demonstrated that she had a healthy temper of her own beneath the poised and unflappable mask she usually wore.

It was dark outside, and in the dull light of the dashboard Gabriel could just see the fine curve of her jaw, and the corner of her mouth, compressed into a cross line. By rights, she should have had frosty blue eyes to match her manner, he thought, but Tess's eyes hadn't looked like that at all. They were clear and brown and dappled with gold, the eyes of someone warm and alluring, and not those of the PA who treated him with such icy civility. Gabriel was unnerved by how vividly he could picture them still.

Irritably, he flexed his shoulders. He had only looked into Tess's eyes for a matter of seconds. Nothing had changed. She was just sitting there with her nose stuck in the air, so why should he suddenly find her so distracting?

He didn't have time to be distracted, he reminded himself roughly. Taking over SpaceWorks had been a risky strategy, and if they didn't get the Emery contract, he would have lost his gamble, not to mention a lot of money. Gabriel didn't like losing. He wasn't going to jeopardise the whole bid by letting himself get diverted by a baby, and certainly not because his secretary had taken her glasses off!

Harry was asleep by the time they drew up outside Tess's house almost an hour later, so Gabriel waited in the car with him while she ran inside and threw a few things for the night into a bag. Then they had to turn round and crawl back through the traffic to the City where Gabriel lived in a recently converted warehouse near the river.

Tess was fed up of sitting in the car by the time they got there and, when she saw his flat, she wished that she had suggested they simply stay at her house, which might be shabby but which at least had the advantage of being comfortable. She had thought about making the offer when she'd been packing her bag, but her home was her haven, and she wasn't sure she wanted Gabriel there.

His apartment was aggressively modern, all gleaming steel and glass and neutral fabrics. Cosy, it was not. Open-plan throughout, the various living areas were cleverly suggested by the arrangement of furniture or lighting. It was chic, stylish and completely soulless. Tess couldn't imagine anyone actually *living* in it. As it was, Harry's pram with its bright, plastic colours struck a jarring note amongst all that restrained taste.

Perhaps it was just as well she hadn't invited Gabriel to stay with her, she decided. If this was his style, he would have hated her house.

'It's very…new,' she said.

'You don't like it.' Too late, Gabriel heard the accusing note in his voice, which made him sound almost as if he cared what she thought.

'It's not that. It's just doesn't have much character, I suppose.'

'I don't want character,' he said tersely. 'I want convenience. These apartments have been snapped up. They all come fully equipped with sheets, towels, crockery, even a selection of wine in the wine rack. They're ideal for successful people who don't have time to waste finding somewhere to buy a corkscrew.'

Tess was unimpressed. 'I don't think I'd want to be successful if it meant I didn't have time to make a home,' she said.

'Home is just somewhere to sleep.'

Nettled by her lack of enthusiasm, Gabriel went to draw the vertical blinds over the expanse of glass that stretched almost the entire length of the apartment. He hadn't noticed it until now, but when it was dark outside and the rain was splattering against the window like now, the apartment didn't look very welcoming. Perhaps she would appreciate it more if he shut out the blackness.

'I only moved in two days ago,' he said, looking for some way to pull the blinds. He liked the view at night, so he hadn't had to work out how to close them before. 'I was living in a hotel until then,' he went on as his hand moved up and down the edge of the blind in search of a cord or some kind of mechanism, 'but this is much better. It's serviced in the same way as a hotel, but it's private and, because it's new, everything works.'

'Not quite everything,' said Tess, observing his increasingly frustrated efforts to deal with the blinds. He was muttering under his breath, and looked ready to rip the blinds bodily from the window as she moved him aside. 'Here, let me try.'

To Gabriel's intense irritation, she located the high-tech controls straight away that had been cleverly concealed in the wall, and with one touch of a button the blinds swished smoothly across the vast window.

'Very convenient,' she murmured.

Gabriel glared at the irony in her voice, but Harry was making little mewling noises from the pram.

'He's waking up,' said Tess nervously.

Drawn together insensibly by their shared apprehension, they peered into the pram, where the baby was squirming and knuckling his eyes.

'Now what do we do?' asked Gabriel, keeping a cautious distance.

Tess pulled Bella's instructions out of her bag. 'I think we need to feed him,' she said, squinting in an attempt to decipher a squiggle in the margin. 'We've got to make up some formula,' she added, hoping that she sounded more confident than she felt. Crouching down, she searched through the equipment that Gabriel had carried up from the car. 'There should be a tin…ah, that must be it.'

'Are you sure you know what you're doing?' said Gabriel suspiciously as he followed her into the kitchen area.

'No.' She held out her scribbled notes with a challenging look. 'If you can read my shorthand, you're welcome to try and work it out for yourself.'

'No, no,' he said, recoiling. 'You'd better do it.'

Tess was reading the instructions on the back of the tin. 'Can you find me a saucepan?'

'I expect I could manage that,' said Gabriel with dignity, still smarting over his defeat with the blinds. He began opening cupboards, having ignored the kitchen, like the windows, until now. Eventually he found a pan and gave it to Tess, who sent him back to keep an eye on Harry.

'This is complicated,' she told him frankly. 'I can't concentrate with you standing over me.'

Harry grew increasingly restless as Gabriel hovered by the pram, watching anxiously as the little face contorted itself into a variety of plaintive expressions, each of which looked alarmingly as if he was on the point of wailing miserably.

When he did finally utter a spluttering cry, Gabriel threw a glance of appeal at Tess, who was carefully measuring powder into a jug. 'Is his milk ready yet?'

'No, I've still got to warm it,' she said, throwing Harry a harassed glance. 'You'll have to distract him.'

'How?'

'I don't know…give him a cuddle or something.'

With a sigh, Gabriel hoisted Harry awkwardly against his shoulder and joggled him about a bit. 'It's not working,' he complained when the baby's cries only increased in volume.

'I'm not surprised.' Tess looked up from the hob where she was puzzling over a control panel that wouldn't have looked out of place at NASA. 'Is that your idea of a cuddle?'

'What's wrong with it?' he said stiffly.

'Nothing, if you think cuddling means holding someone at arm's length and shaking them up and down.'

'I didn't realise you were such an expert,' he said with a snide look.

'I'm not,' she said, 'but I know how I like to be held.'

She didn't have to say that it wouldn't be the way *he* would hold her. 'Perhaps you should give lessons,' snapped Gabriel, unaccountably provoked. He could imagine her doing it, too, with the same cold efficiency she did everything else. No doubt she would allot special cuddling windows in her diary and keep one eye firmly on the clock to make sure they didn't run over schedule.

'Lessons would be extra,' Tess snapped back, 'and I'm already on double overtime this evening.'

'Don't worry, I hadn't forgotten,' said Gabriel sourly.

Grudgingly, he held Harry a little closer and walked up and down in what he hoped was a soothing manner. Not that it made the slightest difference to the volume of the baby's crying. So much for Tess and her advice on cuddling.

'What's taking so long?' he demanded at last, breaking the hostile silence. 'It's only milk, isn't it? Anyone would think you were preparing a five-course meal.'

Tess gritted her teeth. 'I'm being as quick as I can. I've got to check the temperature before I can give it to him.'

Craning her neck to refer to her scribbled notes, she shook the bottle and upended it to squeeze a few drops of milk onto the inside of her wrist. It felt just warm, but not hot, just as Bella had said it should.

Relieved, Tess looked around for somewhere to sit, but it wasn't the kind of kitchen designed to be cluttered up with tables where you could read the paper, drink coffee, let things pile up and generally gather mess. The chairs set perfectly around the glass dining table looked downright uncomfortable, and in the end she sat down a little dubiously on one of the cream sofas.

'OK, let's try him with this.'

Gabriel handed a bawling Harry over with relief. Tess pretended not to notice when their hands brushed, and concentrated on presenting the baby with the bottle. Fortunately, Harry knew more about bottle-feeding than she did and, once he recognised the teat, he soon settled into sucking.

Their sniping momentarily forgotten, Tess and Gabriel watched warily, and were just allowing themselves to relax when he coughed and choked milk down the front of his Babygro. Too late, Tess remembered the bibs that had been tucked in a bag with the nappies.

'What's happening?' said Gabriel.

'*I* don't know, do I?' Tess sat Harry upright and patted his back, which seemed to be the right thing to do, for he stopped spluttering. Cautiously, she let him have the bottle again. 'I'd no idea what a tense business it was looking after a baby.' She sighed.

'Me neither,' Gabriel agreed with feeling. He had taken off his jacket and was standing at the glass table, loosening his tie with one hand and pulling papers from his briefcase with the other. 'Give me executive stress any day!'

'I wouldn't have thought that was something *you* suffered from,' said Tess and Gabriel glanced up at her with a frown.

'What do you mean?'

'No one could call your management style relaxed,' she pointed out, thinking of the last frantic weeks putting the Emery bid together. 'You only seem to operate under high pressure.' She bent her head back over the peacefully suckling baby. 'I'm surprised you even know what executive stress *is*!'

'Of course I know what it is,' said Gabriel irritably. 'I hear my executives whining about it often enough! It's not something I've got a lot of time for, I admit.'

'Not everyone thrives under pressure the way you do,' said Tess. 'You have no idea what it's like to work in an office where the pace is relentless, where the boss storms around making unreasonable demands of his staff and everything always has to be done yesterday.'

Gabriel's fearsome brows twitched together. Looking up from his papers again, he found his gaze resting on her bent head, the brown hair caught the light and gleaming with gold, reminding him of her eyes. He could see the pure line of her cheek, the downward sweep of lashes, that small but stubborn chin.

He wrenched his eyes away. 'It doesn't seem to bother *you*.'

Tess glanced up briefly and then away. 'I cope with it,' she said. 'That doesn't mean I like it.'

'You don't have to like it,' said Gabriel, reverting to his brusque manner to disguise the sensation that had stirred so strangely inside him as he watched her cradling the baby in her arms. 'You just have to do the job you're paid to do, and that's helping me put the Emery bid together. Once we get that in, you can start worrying about stress! Until then, we've got better things to do.'

He glanced at his watch. 'We ought to be able to get quite a bit done tonight. I've got to redraft the introduction, and I want you to cross-check every single figure we put forward. There's going to be some stiff competition for this contract, and we can't afford to look sloppy.'

'You want me to check figures tonight?' said Tess incredulously.

'I am paying you overtime,' Gabriel reminded her.

'For helping you with Harry!'

He brushed that aside. 'Since you're here, you might as well help me with the bid, too. There's no TV, no books. There's just you, me, and a whole heap of paperwork. What else is there for us to do this evening, after all?'

The sardonic note in his voice brought a flush to Tess's cheeks. Most men and women could find something better to do with an evening alone together, but she and Gabriel didn't have that kind of relationship, did they? They might be alone in his apartment with the whole night ahead of them, but he was still her boss and she was still his PA.

'In the circumstances, nothing,' she agreed stiffly.

'You don't have to help,' said Gabriel with an indifferent shrug. 'It's up to you if you want to lose your job.'

Tess's head jerked up and she stared icily at him. 'Is that a threat?'

'No, it's not a threat.' Gabriel's voice was flat and hard and as cold as her own. 'It's reality. We need this contract. If we don't get it, I'm going to have to reconsider my investment in SpaceWorks. In that case, the company will fold, and your job with it. It's as simple as that. Contraxa is a leader in its field, and our reputation depends on consistent quality and success. We can't afford to be associated with failures, even in a minor division.'

Tess knew that what he said was true, but she couldn't help bridling at his casual dismissal of the company where she had worked so loyally for over ten years. SpaceWorks was more than a *minor division*! 'I wonder you bothered with us at all if we're that unimportant!' she said tightly.

'Because I believe in taking risks to get what you want,' said Gabriel. He dropped the last of the papers from his briefcase onto the table where they landed with a dull slap. 'SpaceWorks isn't important now, but it's got the potential to be very important indeed. If my gamble pays off, it will give me the toe-hold I need to expand into Europe. It's a global market now, Tess. You've got to stay ahead of the game, and you don't do that by playing safe.'

'Sometimes playing safe is the only option.' Tess sighed a little, thinking of Andrew with still another year to go before he finished his education. 'Some of us have got commitments. We can't all afford to take risks.'

'That's why I avoid making commitments,' said Gabriel dismissively. 'You can't succeed if you're always looking over your shoulder, worrying about your responsibilities.'

It was all very well for him, thought Tess crossly, removing the empty bottle from Harry's tenacious grasp. Some commitments were there whether chosen or not.

She put the bottle on the floor and stood up with Harry. 'Well, here's one responsibility you can worry about right now,' she said, deliberately brisk. 'You can take your nephew for a while.'

CHAPTER THREE

GABRIEL eyed the baby Tess was holding out to him. 'What shall I do with him?' he asked uneasily, his high-handed indifference abruptly deserting him.

'According to Bella, he needs to be winded. I've seen her husband do this,' Tess said, relenting in the face of his panic-stricken expression. 'It's easy. All you have to do is walk up and down, patting his back until he burps.'

Gabriel felt that he had already done quite enough walking up and down with Harry but, since Tess had fed him, he couldn't really refuse. Stretching out his arms reluctantly, he let her put the baby into them.

'Got him?' she asked sharply to disguise the inexplicable frisson of awareness as her hands brushed against his again.

'Yes,' he admitted, although without much enthusiasm.

'Now, hold him against your shoulder, and pat his back—gently.'

Gabriel patted gingerly. 'Like this?'

'Well, Roger sings while he's at it,' said Tess as she went into the kitchen to rinse the bottle, 'but I think that's optional.'

She watched Gabriel under her lashes as she dragged the steriliser out from under the pram and unpacked it from its box. Face intent, he was walking dutifully around the apartment with Harry. If only the others at SpaceWorks could see him now, the ruthless arrogance and uncompromising confidence demolished by one small baby.

Sometimes, thought Tess, life could be sweet.

Completing another circuit, Gabriel arrived back in the kitchen. 'I think I'm beginning to get the hang of it,' he confided, and ventured a hum to demonstrate his new-found confidence.

Harry was promptly sick over his extremely expensive shirt.

Yes, definitely sweet, decided Tess, hiding a smile. Even perfect.

'You *were* a bit out of tune,' she reproached him.

Gabriel shot her a look as he craned his neck over his shoulder to assess the damage. 'That's all I need,' he said sourly. 'A critic.'

Tess hunted through the pristine cupboards for a cloth, eventually locating an unopened packet which she ripped open. 'That must be why Roger always wears a cloth over his shoulder when he winds Rosy,' she said, extracting one and wetting it under the tap.

'I'm so pleased you remembered that now,' he grumbled.

Ignoring him, Tess wrung out the cloth and put a hand on his arm. 'Stand still,' she instructed. She wiped away the mess on his shoulder, but she had barely finished before Harry obligingly gugged up a little more milk.

Gabriel screwed up his nose. 'Yeuch!'

'Oh, don't make such a fuss.' she said, half-exasperated, half-indulgent. 'It's only a bit of milk.' She rubbed his shirt vigorously. 'There…all gone.'

He peered suspiciously at the unpleasantly damp patch behind his shoulder before raising his gaze to meet Tess's. The honey-coloured eyes were dancing with amusement, and Gabriel felt as if his stomach had disappeared without warning, leaving him with a strange, hollow feeling inside. All at once he was acutely conscious of Tess standing close beside him, of her hand burning through the fine material of his shirt, of her hair, glimmering in the glare of the overhead light, of her perfume, elusive, beguiling, faintly spicy.

At almost exactly the same moment, Tess became aware

of the solid strength of the shoulder she was dabbing in such a casual manner. The arm she had taken hold of so intimately was *warm*, and she had a sudden, shocking sense of him as a man. A man with steely muscles and sleek, bare flesh beneath his clothes. Unaccountably flustered, she jerked her hand away and stepped back.

'I'll...er...I'll see what we have to do next,' she muttered.

Her fingers were not quite steady as she smoothed out Bella's instructions on the kitchen worktop. Really, she had to get a grip. She had never found Gabriel remotely attractive before, and she wasn't about to start now.

Tess concentrated on the notes. 'There's something here about a bath,' she said after a moment, glad to hear that her voice sounded almost normal again. 'I wonder if we should have done that before feeding him? It's a bit hard to tell from this.'

In the end, they decided that it wouldn't hurt Harry to miss a bath for one night. The nanny would be able to wash him the next day and in the meantime wiping him with a flannel, changing his nappy and buttoning him into a clean Babygro presented enough of a challenge for them.

'Let's put him in here.' Gabriel snapped on a light by a low, wide bed set against the far wall of the apartment. To one side, a wall of glass gave a spectacular view over the city lights, while a range of wardrobes curved round like a protective arm, providing privacy from the rest of the apartment.

Tess looked around her, noting the gleaming bathroom to one side. It, at least, had a door. Apart from the front door, it appeared to be the only one in the apartment.

'Is this where you sleep?'

'Yes.' Now that he knew how they worked, Gabriel went over to pull the blinds over the window, but something in the quality of Tess's silence made him turn. 'Not tonight, however. You needn't worry,' he went on in a dry voice. 'You'll have the bed to yourself. I'll sleep on the couch.'

Tess flushed a little. 'I wasn't worrying,' she said, lifting her chin in a familiar gesture. 'I was simply thinking that you wouldn't be very comfortable.' The sofas were luxuriously wide, but he was well over six foot with a massive strength that she couldn't imagine fitting very easily onto the cream cushions.

He shrugged. 'It's not a problem.'

'I don't mind sleeping on the sofa,' she offered hesitantly. 'I'm shorter than you.'

Gabriel had been opening and closing wardrobe doors, but he paused at that and looked over his shoulder at her. 'I realise you have a very low opinion of me, Tess,' he said with some asperity, 'but I didn't know it was quite that low. Do you really think I would let you sleep on the couch while I was warm and comfortable in bed?'

Tess bit her lip as he turned back to continue rifling through the wardrobes. She would have been surprised if he had accepted her offer, it was true, but there had been no need for him to make her feel ridiculous for even suggesting it.

'What are you looking for?' she asked awkwardly instead of answering him.

'Clean bedding,' said Gabriel briefly. He shut the last door with a frown. 'I can't find anything. I guess the bed gets changed as part of the service here, but that won't be for a couple of days.'

'It doesn't matter,' she said, trying not to think about sleeping in his bed, in his sheets.

'The sheets are quite clean,' he said stiffly, certain that she was notching up another black mark against the convenience of his new apartment. Everything had worked perfectly until she had arrived. 'I've only spent one night here.'

Where had he spent the other night? wondered Tess involuntarily. *Two* days ago, he had said he'd moved in. Then she remembered Fionnula Jenkins. No doubt he had been with her, and not sleeping on her sofa either!

'I'll be fine,' she said, rocking Harry with a fine show of nonchalance. She certainly wasn't about to let Gabriel Stearne know that the very idea of sleeping in his bed, in his sheets, left her feeling curiously ruffled.

Harry wasn't keen on being left alone in a strange room, and made his feelings known in no uncertain terms. Every time Tess and Gabriel made to creep out, he would set up a desolate wail that brought them hastily back to his side. They were just beginning to wonder if they were going to have to spend the entire evening hanging over his pram when exhaustion got the better of him, in spite of his valiant struggles to keep his eyes open.

Holding their breaths, they watched as his long, baby lashes flickered, drooped and lifted manfully twice, three times, four and then rested against the downy cheeks. Tess saw his tiny fists relax as his breathing grew slow and steady at last, and she nodded when Gabriel turned up his thumbs with a hopeful look.

Together, they tiptoed out into the living area.

'What an evening!' muttered Gabriel, raking his fingers tiredly through his dark hair.

Tess collapsed onto one of the cream sofas. 'I know.' She sighed with feeling. 'How do you think parents do that every night?'

'God knows!' he said bitterly as he lay back opposite her and closed his eyes. 'All I know is that if I had ever wanted children, this little experience would have changed my mind.'

Easing off her shoes, Tess massaged her feet and wondered if it would be OK if she took her tights off later. Without thinking, she pulled the clips from her hair and shook it loose with a stifled yawn, the way she did every night as soon as she got home.

'I don't think I'll be giving up my job to train as a nanny either,' she said, obscurely comforted to realise that Gabriel was as tired as she was.

'I'm glad to hear—' Gabriel began dryly, only to stop short as he opened his eyes to see Tess curled up on his sofa, massaging her feet, luxuriant brown hair tumbling to her shoulders. He blinked, stunned by the transformation. Where had all that hair come from? It made her look like a different girl altogether, no longer cool and remote, but warm, vibrant and sexy.

Sexy? *Tess?*

The thought made him jerk upright.

Startled by his sudden movement, Tess pushed back her hair and looked at him in concern. 'What is it?'

Gabriel opened his mouth and closed it again. 'What about a drink?' he said, getting abruptly to his feet and hoping that Tess wouldn't notice the hoarseness of his voice. 'I don't know about you, but I could sure use one tonight.'

Escaping to the kitchen, he took longer than strictly necessary to find the corkscrew and open a bottle of wine. The sight of Tess with her hair loose and her long legs curled comfortably up beneath her had caught him unawares. He hadn't realised she could look like that, and he just needed a few minutes to adjust, that was all.

He had himself well under control by the time he carried the bottle and two glasses back to the sofa. 'There's nothing to eat in the apartment,' he told Tess, 'so I've ordered in a pizza. Is that OK?'

'A *pizza*?'

Gabriel raised his eyebrows at her expression as he poured the wine into the glasses. 'What's the matter? Don't you like pizza?'

'Pizza's fine,' said Tess. 'I'm just surprised at the idea of you ordering a take-away,' she tried to explain. 'I suppose I think of you always eating in smart restaurants like

Cupiditas.' She broke off as Gabriel swore and slapped his palm to his forehead. 'What have I said?' she asked, puzzled.

'You've just reminded me that I'm supposed to be having dinner there tonight.'

'I thought you would have cancelled,' said Tess. She had taken the opportunity to ring her friends when she'd been packing her bag at home, and assumed that Gabriel would have done the same while he'd been waiting in the car.

'I had other things on my mind.' Gabriel felt for his mobile before remembering that he had left it in the kitchen. He got up. 'I'd better ring Fionnula.'

Leaning back against the cushions, Tess sipped her wine and wondered just what kind of relationship he had with Fionnula Jenkins. It couldn't be that close if Gabriel had forgotten her so completely.

From the kitchen she could hear the murmur of Gabriel's voice. Grovelling apologies wouldn't come easily to him, and it sounded as if Fionnula was giving him a hard time. Tess couldn't imagine the beautiful redhead would get stood up very often. She had better get used to it if she was planning on spending much time with a workaholic like Gabriel, thought Tess cynically. He wasn't the type to change his habits for anyone.

Sure enough, Gabriel was looking boot-faced when he came back from the kitchen a few minutes later, snapping his mobile closed. Fionnula had been furious to learn that she had been stood up in favour of a baby, and aghast when Gabriel had told her that he'd had to take responsibility for Harry on behalf of his brother.

'You realise that everyone's going to think that it's your baby?' she had said angrily.

'Nobody's going to know, and if they did know, they're not going to be interested,' he'd told her impatiently.

'Easy for you to say. You're not a celebrity over here.

I don't suppose you gave a thought to what it might do to my reputation if it leaked out that you had a secret love child?'

Since Gabriel hadn't, it had been hard for him to deny it. Fionnula had not been impressed, and he'd been hard put to it to control his temper. Now, his jaw worked angrily as he took a slug of his wine.

'Come on, we might as well start work while we're waiting for the pizza to arrive,' he said.

At least she wasn't the one who had put him in a bad mood for once, thought Tess, reaching resignedly for the first set of papers.

They sat down together at the dining table, but the chairs had clearly been designed for show rather than for sitting on, and it wasn't long before they decamped back to the sofas by mutual agreement. Gabriel sat on the edge, leaning forward to study the report on the coffee table, while Tess found a comfortable position on the floor.

For a while they worked in a silence that felt almost companionable. Tess worked her way methodically through the figures, checking each set against the originals. Every now and then she stopped to take a sip of wine or push her hair behind her ears so that she could adjust the glasses on her nose, but as the minutes ticked past for some reason she became increasingly aware of Gabriel.

He was sitting opposite her, leaning his elbows on his knees, sleeves rolled up to reveal strong forearms, and brows drawn together in concentration. Without that acute grey gaze boring into her, Tess could study him under her lashes. The dark, stern face with its intimidating brows was familiar to her, but she had never noticed the scattering of grey hairs at his temples before, nor the lines fanning out from the corner of his eyes.

He was rubbing a finger thoughtfully along his upper lip and Tess found herself remembering how he had looked when he'd smiled at Harry. Worse, she found herself wondering what it would be like if he smiled at *her*.

The realisation made her shift uncomfortably, breaking Gabriel's concentration. He glanced across at her. 'How's it going?'

'OK.' Tess was alarmed to hear the squeak in her voice, and she cleared her throat hastily. 'I've done last year's figures.'

'Good.'

Gabriel's eyes flickered towards her, then away. He wondered if Tess had any idea how disconcerting it was to see her sitting casually on the floor with her hair falling to her shoulders. She had taken off her jacket and was wearing a short-sleeved top in a silky ivory material with a string of pearls at her neck. It was exactly the kind of classic outfit she wore every day, so why did she suddenly look so *different*?

He tried to go back to his report, but it was impossible to concentrate. An indefinable tension had trickled into the atmosphere, making the print jiggle before his eyes, and it was a relief when the pizza finally arrived and gave them an excuse to push the papers to one side.

Tess opened up the box on the coffee table, while Gabriel poured her another glass of wine. She was so hungry by then that she was beginning to feel light-headed, and it didn't even seem strange any more to be sitting on the floor in Gabriel's trendy apartment, eating pizza out of cardboard box.

Afterwards, Gabriel made coffee. 'There's no milk, I'm afraid,' he said as he handed her a mug, but I found these in the fridge.' He indicated the box of luxurious Belgian chocolates tucked under his arm. 'I think they must have been left as a welcoming gift. 'Do you eat chocolates?'

'Occasionally,' said Tess, who was a closet chocaholic. She eyed the box longingly as Gabriel set it down on the coffee table.

'Be my guest,' he said.

'Thanks.' Tess wasn't about to give him the chance to change his mind. Reaching for the box, she tried not to look too eager as she unwrapped the Cellophane and lifted the lid with reverence.

She pored over the chocolates, her fingers hovering with anticipation before finally making her selection, and popping it into her mouth with a sigh of pleasure. 'My favourites,' she confessed through a mouthful of chocolate.

Gabriel lifted an eyebrow. 'Have another,' he offered. 'Have the whole box!'

For once, the irony went over Tess's head. She was too busy choosing another chocolate. Oblivious to the curious expression in Gabriel's eyes, she settled her glasses comfortably back on her nose and went back to her figures, absently eating her way through the entire box.

'What's wrong with that one?' asked Gabriel some time later when they paused to stretch stiff muscles.

Tess had taken off her glasses and was running her fingers through her hair, pulling it back from her face. 'Which one?' she asked blankly.

For answer, Gabriel upended the box to reveal a solitary chocolate nestling in an expanse of packaging.

'It's got nougat in it,' she explained. 'I don't like nougat.'

'Nor do I.'

'You did say I could have the whole box,' she reminded him, faintly defensive.

'I didn't think you'd take me literally.' said Gabriel, but the corner of his mouth twitched.

'You shouldn't have said it if you didn't mean it.'

'Obviously not,' he said dryly, regarding her with such a peculiar expression that Tess began to feel uncomfortable.

'Why are you looking at me like that?'

'I was just thinking that you're quite…' He searched for

the right word. 'Quite unexpected,' was the best that he could do.

It was hardly a lavish compliment—it might not even have been meant as a compliment at all—but Tess felt her heart tighten. It wasn't what Gabriel had said. It was something to do with a new charge in the air, with the jittery, uncertain feeling that was stealing over her, as if she had strayed unknowingly onto dangerous ground.

She moistened her lips. 'Most people like chocolates. What's unexpected about that?'

'It's not the fact that you like chocolate. It's the fact that you just ate a whole box,' said Gabriel. 'Normally you're so restrained, so controlled.'

Tess put up her chin, not really liking the image that he had conjured up, but knowing that was how she came across. 'I am, in the office.' She allowed that much.

'And out of it?'

Gabriel's voice was light, laced with mockery, but when Tess glanced involuntarily at him she found her eyes trapped by his, and she was paralysed by a sudden, absurd shyness. There was something in his expression that held her still while her senses sharpened to an acuteness that made her catch her breath, and she was startlingly aware of the lingering taste of chocolate in her mouth, of the faint stickiness on her fingers, of the sound of her own heartbeat.

And of Gabriel.

Of the dent at the corner of his stern mouth. Of the crease in his cheeks. Of the pulse beating slowly in his throat.

Shaken, Tess dragged her gaze away. What on earth was the matter with her?

'I'm just the same out of the office,' she managed to say. 'I just eat more chocolate.'

She'd hoped to sound suitably crisp, but there was a treacherously breathless note to her voice, and when she picked up her coffee the cup rattled so much in the saucer that she had to put it down again.

Pushing her hair behind her ears in an unconsciously nervous gesture, Tess drew a breath and fumbled for her glasses. 'We...we'd better get on.'

She felt better with her glasses on. They made her once more the cool, capable PA Gabriel believed her to be, and not the kind of girl whose heart lurched alarmingly at his smile. Not the kind of girl who couldn't tear her eyes away from his.

Certainly not the kind of girl who stared at his mouth and wondered what it would take to convince him that her crisp efficiency was just a façade and that underneath she was warm and sensual and passionate.

Not that she *was* that kind of girl, of course.

Not with her glasses on, anyway.

After that it was even harder to concentrate. There was a new constraint to the silence between them and Tess was excruciatingly aware of Gabriel's every move, tensing each time he turned a page or leant forward to make a neat note in the margin. The figures kept dancing in front of her eyes and blurring into the image of his face.

Tiredness, Tess told herself firmly.

Struggling to the end of the file, she dropped it onto the coffee table and leant back with a sigh that turned into a yawn as she linked her hands above her head and stretched her arms.

Gabriel looked at his watch. It was nearly midnight. 'Go to bed,' he said brusquely.

'I've still got two more files to check.'

'You've done enough for tonight. Go on, go.'

'What about the bid?'

'We'll do the rest tomorrow,' he said.

'But—'

'Stop arguing,' said Gabriel crossly to disguise an unfamiliar feeling of guilt. Apart from a few minutes break to eat the pizza, Tess had been working all evening, and she looked very tired. 'You'll be no good to me tomorrow if you're half asleep.'

Putting his hand under her arm, he lifted her bodily to her feet and propelled her towards the bedroom. Tess was too stiff and weary by then to resist the warm strength of the hand gripping her arm. Swaying tiredly, she checked that Harry was still sleeping while Gabriel grabbed some shorts and a T-shirt out of a drawer.

He turned to see her sitting on the edge of the bed, looking blankly ahead of her as if too exhausted to get undressed. 'Will you be all right?' he asked, rough concern in his voice.

'I'll be fine.'

'I'll say goodnight, then.' Gabriel hesitated, as if he were about to say more but, whatever it was, he evidently changed his mind, contenting himself with a curt nod of farewell instead.

Tess slid beneath the duvet and lay with her eyes closed. It was dark and quiet and she was very tired, but she couldn't sleep. Her body was strumming, the nerves fluttering beneath her skin. It was something to do with being in Gabriel's bed, something to do with remembering the lean, powerful body and the way his face had changed when he smiled at Harry.

Something to do with the feel of his hand on her arm.

Unthinkingly, she rubbed the inside of her arm where he had gripped her, and where her skin was tingling as if his fingers were imprinted on her like a burn. She hadn't realised how strong he was, nor how warm his hands would be.

The thought made Tess shift uneasily. She loved expensive lingerie and only ever wore silk or satin to bed, but now for some reason its sensuous softness made her uncomfortable and all too aware of her own nakedness. If only she possessed one of those Victorian nightgowns that enveloped her from neck to toe, instead of this slithery satin number which left her arms and shoulders bare. It made it too easy to imagine that she could feel the warmth of his body on the sheet beneath her.

Restlessly, Tess turned over and buried her face in the pillow, but that didn't help at all. The cool linen held the scent of his skin, of his hair. How had she come to recognise it so unmistakably? It was almost like having him in bed with her.

And *that* thought didn't help her relax either.

Tess pummelled the pillow and rolled onto her back once more with an irritable sigh. This was ridiculous. She didn't even *like* Gabriel. He was rude, surly, selfish, and an impossibly demanding boss—the last person she was prepared to lose any sleep over, in fact. If she had to lie awake, she should be calculating the overtime she had already earned this evening.

Somewhere in the middle of working out her hourly rate and trying to multiply it by two, Tess fell asleep.

She didn't know how long she slept, but it felt like mere moments before she was jerked awake by a piercing wail. Disorientated, she lay with her heart pumping in alarm before she remembered where she was.

Gabriel's apartment.

A baby. Crying.

Get up and do something about it.

Fumbling for the bedside light, she screwed up her eyes as she clicked it on and stumbled over to the pram.

What had Bella said about sleeping patterns? Tess couldn't remember. She tried rocking the pram, and when that didn't work, bent to pick Harry up. He was tense and miserable, his small body arching away from hers and his arms flailing wildly in distress.

A light snapped on in the living area, and the next minute Gabriel appeared, rubbing a hand wearily over his face. He looked cross and rumpled, but the sight of him was enough to snap Tess back to full consciousness in a way that Harry's screams hadn't done.

Averting her eyes from his long, straight, strong legs and the breadth of his chest beneath the T-shirt he wore, she cuddled Harry against her, patting his back and attempting the kind of croon she had heard Bella use. He resisted at first, before the taut little body relaxed slightly, but the heart-rending sobs continued.

'Can I do anything?'

Gabriel's voice sounded a bit odd, but perhaps he was feeling as befuddled as she was. Tess forced herself to think about what Bella had said. 'Could you get his bottle?' she asked. 'I got it ready earlier. Maybe he just wants something to drink.' She knew she was clutching at straws, but it was the only useful thing she could think of to do.

Gabriel nodded briefly and turned towards the kitchen. The sight of Tess, warm from the bed, with her hair dishevelled, and that seductive nightdress skimming lovingly over the curve of breast and hip had hit him with the force of a blow. He was glad to escape and give himself time to recover and remember how to breathe.

He had himself under control by the time he returned with the bottle. Harry's cries had subsided as Tess cradled him and, although he drank a little, he didn't seem very interested. When his eyes started to droop once more, Tess lowered him gently back into the pram.

Her eyes met Gabriel's as she straightened. The bedside lamp cast a soft puddle of light, and she was very glad of the shadows, but they didn't stop her feeling very conscious once more of how little she had on. She hugged her arms together nervously.

'Perhaps he'll go back to sleep now,' she said hopefully, holding up crossed fingers.

He did, but only for a few minutes. Barely had Tess dropped back into sleep than Harry woke again.

And again. And again. And again.

It set the pattern for a night that rapidly turned into a nightmare for Tess. They tried everything they could think of to get Harry back to sleep. They made up some milk. They walked him up and down patting his back. They sang to him. They even changed his nappy, and none of it made any difference. No sooner had they plummeted into an exhausted sleep than the screams would start again.

After the third time, they agreed that they would take it in turns to get up to him. By that stage, they were beyond caring or even noticing how little the other was wearing. Tess had lost track of time altogether. It was as if she and Gabriel were subjects in some awful trial on the effects of torture, and Harry had been specifically programmed to deny them the sleep they craved.

She surfaced groggily at one point to see Gabriel cautiously laying Harry in his pram, and turning back towards his sofa.

'You might as well stay here,' she mumbled, her voice blurred by sleep, and her arm gestured vaguely to the other side of the bed. 'There's plenty of room.'

Gabriel hesitated. He was rather more awake than Tess at that point and, although it was a very tempting idea, he wasn't sure that it was a good one. 'Are you sure you don't mind?' he whispered so as not to wake the baby.

'Mmm… Stupid going back to sofa when you're only going to have to come back again.' She was slurring her words, barely conscious. ''s nice and warm…'

Nice and warm. Gabriel swallowed. He could believe it.

He watched Tess roll over and burrow her face in her pillow, and grimaced. She was already asleep, and too tired to care where he slept. He knew perfectly well that she hadn't known what she was saying, but it did make sense. He was sick of going backwards and forwards. The couch was cold and uncomfortable, and the bed looked very inviting.

Carefully, he lifted the duvet and slid in beside Tess. In

spite of his own exhaustion, he was dangerously aware of her, slumbering, oblivious to his presence only inches away. He could feel the soft warmth of her body, and hear her slow breathing.

Moving right to the edge of the bed, he turned his back to her and prayed for sleep.

Gabriel surfaced slowly to the feel of a warm, female body nestled into the hard curve of his. She was utterly relaxed. His arm lay half over her, moving gently up and down in time with her quiet breathing. There was some soft, slithery material beneath his hand where it rested on her thigh and his face was pressed into a mass of silky hair that smelt clean and sweet and familiar.

He was warm and comfortable. Still half asleep, Gabriel was conscious only that it felt right to be lying there, and he tightened his arm around her. When the slinky material slipped tantalisingly over her skin, pulling her into him was a purely instinctive response.

She stirred, and rolled sleepily within his arm to nuzzle against him. Gabriel twisted his hands in the thick hair and kissed her throat, smiling as he shifted her beneath him and let his lips drift deliciously up to her jaw. The sleep had cleared from his brain, but he wasn't thinking. He was simply reacting to her softness and her warmth, to the enticing feel of her body and the beguiling scent of her skin.

Murmuring inarticulate pleasure, she wound her arms around his neck. Still smiling, Gabriel lifted his head to look down into her face.

And froze.

CHAPTER FOUR

DRAWN blissfully up from the fathoms of slumber, Tess smiled languorously and opened her eyes. Still clouded with sleep, it took a little while for her to realise that the bewitching drift of his lips had ceased, and that the man leaning over her was looking down at her with an expression of horror.

Gabriel could see the exact second at which the puzzlement in her eyes was blinked away by the sudden, appalling recognition of where they were, and what they were doing. There was a long, paralysing silence while they stared at each other, aghast, and then, at the identical moment, they jerked themselves apart as if a gun had gone off.

'What...what...?' Tess's hammering heart kept missing a stroke, and she struggled upright, frantically trying to clear her head.

What had happened? What was she doing in bed with Gabriel? What was she doing *kissing* Gabriel?

She hadn't actually kissed him, she told herself, grasping desperately at any straw that might somehow make the situation less than excruciatingly, horribly, appallingly embarrassing. Technically, he had been kissing *her*, and even then it hadn't been a real kiss. It wasn't as if their lips had met. When she had slid her arms around his neck, when she had smiled and arched in blissful anticipation as his mouth had drifted towards hers, she hadn't known what she was doing. She hadn't wanted him to kiss her, not really.

She had just been dreaming.

Perhaps she was still dreaming. Perhaps this was just

some terrible nightmare. Tess put her head in her hands and clutched her hair. Please, let it not be real, she prayed.

But it felt real. Her body was booming and twitching as if she could still feel his hand sliding insistently over her hip, his hard, strong body pressing her down into the mattress, the bewitching drift of his lips over her skin. She couldn't have imagined that they would feel that good.

'I'm sorry about that.' Fighting for control, Gabriel had been sitting on the edge of the bed with his back to her, but he turned slightly at last and made himself look at her. 'I don't know what happened there,' he said with an effort.

Tess lifted her head. 'I don't know either,' she said huskily. 'One minute I was dreaming, and the next...' She trailed off as the memory of just what had happened next flamed between them.

'Yes.' Gabriel grimaced. 'I think we must have both been half asleep. I didn't realise I was with you, obviously,' he tried to reassure her.

Obviously? Perversely, Tess stiffened. Why *obviously*? Obviously you're not Fionnula—was that what he was trying to say?

'I'd forgotten what happened last night,' he went on.

Clutching the duvet to her chest, Tess eyed him uneasily. 'What *did* happen?' she asked.

'It was your idea. You invited me to share the bed, and at the time it seemed like a good idea.'

'*I* invited...?' Tess stared at him, appalled. 'When did I do that?'

'About half past five this morning. Don't worry,' Gabriel added ironically, 'it was easily the least flattering invitation I've ever received but, at the time, I had a choice between sleeping with you and sleeping on the couch, and I chose you.'

Tess bit her lip. 'Then, I didn't...?'

'No, you didn't,' said Gabriel in a dry voice. 'You just told me to get in, then rolled over and went back to sleep.

I guess we must have gravitated towards each other in the night—or what was left of it.'

He tried to sound casual, as if it was no big deal and every boss and secretary spent the night together at some stage. He tried not to look at Tess, but somehow his eyes caught hers and held. She was sitting bolt upright in the bed, hugging the duvet to her, and he was very aware of her tumbled hair, of her bare shoulders, of the hollow at the base of her throat where he had kissed her…

With an effort, Gabriel dragged his eyes away and cleared his throat.

'It was just one of those things,' he said gruffly. 'Embarrassing for both of us, but it didn't mean anything.'

Why was it that didn't make her feel any better? Tess wondered.

'No,' she agreed bravely. 'Of course not. Let's forget it.'

Easier said than done, she thought. Being kissed awake by your boss wasn't the kind of thing you could just wipe from your memory, especially not when your skin was still pulsing from the touch of his hands.

Well, she would just have to try and, if she couldn't quite forget, she could at least pretend that she did. She would simply carry on as normal. 'What time is it?'

Good question. Gabriel frowned, noticing the light outside for the first time. He looked at his wrist, but he had left his watch on the coffee table. With the alarm that he had set for six o'clock that morning. There was a sinking feeling in the pit of his stomach as he went through to check.

Groping for her own watch on the bedside table, Tess picked it up just as a muffled curse came from the living area. Half past eight! No wonder Gabriel was furious. He had planned to be in the office an hour ago.

She scrambled out of bed and had a quick shower. When she came out of the bathroom, Gabriel was shoving papers into his attaché case and trying to tighten his tie at the same time.

'No time for breakfast,' he said, after one quick glance at Tess, who was fastening the pearls around her neck. She was wearing the same grey skirt as the day before, with a clean white top. She had gone into the bathroom looking warm and dishevelled, and emerged crisp and businesslike and very much a PA.

How did she do it? Gabriel wondered, momentarily diverted. No one seeing her now would guess that she had been up half the night with a screaming baby.

Nor that she wore satin to bed.

'Are you ready to go?' he asked curtly.

'I am,' said Tess, shrugging on her jacket, 'but what about Harry? He's still asleep.'

'We'll just have to take him with us,' said Gabriel. 'We can't afford to hang around here waiting for him to wake up, and I need you at the office.'

The receptionist's eyebrows crawled into her hairline as she saw Tess and Gabriel coming into the office together, and they nearly disappeared altogether when she spotted the baby. Oblivious to her pantomimed questions behind his back, Gabriel was already working out how to catch up on lost time.

'Get onto an agency and tell them we need a nanny here as soon as possible,' he told Tess as the lift carried them upwards. 'If they can't send someone straight away, see if you can find one of the junior secretaries to look after him until then. I want you to go through the files and make sure all the alterations we checked last night are made on the computer. I'll chase up the legal side.'

He was doing fine, thought Gabriel. Tess was just his PA again. If it hadn't been for the baby she was carrying, he could almost have believed that last night had never happened. And as for this morning, and the softness of her skin and the silkiness of her hair…well, he had practically forgotten it already, he tried to convince himself.

By the time he strode into Tess's office, Gabriel had the day planned out with military precision, plans that were thrown into instant disarray by Harry, who woke up and demanded attention in no uncertain terms the moment Tess sat down at the computer.

The agency Tess rang couldn't get anyone there until lunch-time. Precious time had to be spent changing Harry and then feeding him, and when they tried handing him over to one of the girls from personnel he screamed with such fury that in the end it seemed less trouble to keep him with them.

Having got his own way, and having caught up on all the sleep he had missed the night before, Harry was wide awake and ready to be entertained. Refusing point blank to go back in the pram, he was all smiles when Tess set him on her lap. She did her best, but it was difficult to concentrate on the alterations she was trying to make on the screen when Harry wanted to play with the keyboard too. He thumped at the keys with his dimpled hands and, when Tess moved them away, made a grab instead for the papers she was working from.

Gabriel removed the files and suggested that he read out the alterations, so that Tess didn't have to keep checking between the paper and the screen, and for a while this seemed to work. Harry was distracted by the collection of rulers and pens she'd laid out for him to play with, but it didn't take long for him to put them in his mouth and throw them on the floor, and he was soon reaching enthusiastically for the keyboard once more.

'This is hopeless!' said Gabriel impatiently. 'I'll take him.'

He bent to lift Harry from Tess's lap and, as he did so, he caught the drift of her fragrance, the same scent he had breathed in from her hair when he'd lain in bed beside her.

Straightening abruptly, he stepped away as if from the memory. There were enough distractions to cope with today without him getting diverted by thoughts of last night. *Tess* wasn't distracted. She was wearing the same grey suit she always wore; her hair was neatly tied up; her glasses were on; her fingers, unimpeded by Harry, were flying over the keyboard. She was getting on with the job in hand, not wasting time thinking about last night.

He ought to be pleased to find that she was as efficient as usual, Gabriel knew that, but it didn't stop him feeling vaguely disgruntled. Why should she be able to forget last night, when he couldn't get the feel of her out of his mind? He wanted to be able to concentrate on the bid the way she was doing instead of remembering the warmth of her body beneath his hand, the smooth slither of satin over her skin as she rolled against him, the silky tumble of her hair.

Tess was looking enquiringly at him over the top of her spectacles. Gabriel met her eyes for a moment before belatedly realising that she was waiting for him to continue, and he shifted Harry onto his other arm to cover his discomfiture at having lost his place.

'Read back that last figure,' he barked, avoiding her gaze.

'Ninety-seven thousand,' said Tess without inflection, but Gabriel was certain that she knew that he had been thinking about her.

'Right, ninety-seven thousand.' Gabriel had it now. Feeling an idiot, he began reading his way down the next column of figures. If Tess could pretend that last night had never happened, then so could he. He wasn't even going to mention it.

When they reached the end of the section, Tess began printing out the corrected version and got to her feet. 'Shall I see if Harry's ready for a sleep yet?' she offered.

Taking the baby from Gabriel, she lay him in the pram.

Harry made a few half-hearted protests but, to their relief, it wasn't long before his eyes were drooping.

Perhaps now they would be able to get on, thought Gabriel, exasperated by their slow progress. They still had the rest of the report to print out, and he hadn't checked the appendices yet. He should be working out how best to use the time while Harry was asleep.

'Tess?' he said instead.

She looked up from the pram where she was tucking a blanket around Harry. 'Yes?'

'Am I really the boss from hell?'

What kind of damn fool question was that? Gabriel wondered savagely. The words had slipped out before he had realised what he was saying, and now he was going to look like the kind of employer who actually cared what she thought of him!

Tess's eyes had flown up to meet his for a jarring second before they dropped back to the pram. Carefully, she smoothed the blanket. 'That was just Bella trying to be funny,' she said after a moment, amazed that Gabriel had even remembered.

'She wouldn't have said it if you hadn't told her about me,' he said, even as he told himself the sensible thing would be to let the matter drop right now. But somehow he couldn't.

'Everyone complains about their boss,' Tess prevaricated.

'Did you complain about Steve Robinson?'

Steve had been her boss until Gabriel's arrival. From an upstairs room in Kennington, he had built SpaceWorks into a small but prestigious company that had eventually attracted the attention of Gabriel Stearne. SpaceWorks had been no match for the might of Contraxa. Gabriel had circled like a vulture for eighteen months, swooping down the moment the company had hit a low point, and had annexed SpaceWorks to his empire.

The staff had been stunned by the speed of the takeover, none more so than Tess who had found herself working for the very man who had evicted Steve from the company he loved. No one had expected Gabriel to take charge personally and, with a radical restructuring programme in place, no one wanted him to succeed where Steve had failed. The trouble was that there were an awful lot of people like Tess who weren't in a position to walk out the way they might have wanted. Gabriel's one positive action had been to increase the salaries of those who remained after the drastic downsizing operation. When you had dependants, it was difficult to opt for a cut in pay, no matter how much you might dislike your boss.

'Did you?' Gabriel persisted.

Tess put up her chin. If he was so determined to know the truth, he could have it! 'Not very often, no,' she said. 'We all liked Steve,' she added deliberately. 'He's a very nice man.'

'He may have been nice, but he wasn't effective.' Gabriel was annoyed with himself for starting this conversation. What the hell did it matter to him what Tess thought of him? 'If left to Steve Robinson, SpaceWorks would have been bankrupt within the year, and then you would all have been looking for a new boss anyway.'

'I know Steve wasn't very good at the financial side of things, but he was effective in other ways,' said Tess loyally. 'He could motivate people in a way you would never understand. He knew everybody's name, and made everyone feel important. It didn't matter whether your job was coming up with an original design or just photocopying, Steve would always congratulate you if you'd put a lot of effort into what you were doing.'

'I expect my staff to make an effort as a matter of course,' said Gabriel distantly. 'Why should I congratulate them for doing the jobs they're paid to do?'

'Because they'll work even harder the next time if you

do. It wouldn't kill you to show a little appreciation now and then. You haven't made the slightest effort to get to know the people who work for you.'

He hunched an irritable shoulder. 'I know you.'

'No, you don't.'

'I know you better than I did yesterday,' Gabriel said unfairly, and the air between them reverberated suddenly with the memory of waking up in each other's arms.

Tess flushed and bit back a sharp retort. She didn't want to think about the way they had kissed. Gabriel had no business bringing it up here in the office.

'The point is that the staff here are all loyal to the company,' she said grittily. 'They all want SpaceWorks to succeed, and that's a huge asset to any business. But if you're not careful, you're going to lose it. You could learn a lot from Steve's management style.'

Gabriel's black brows snapped together. 'Oh, you think so, do you?' he said dangerously, but Tess refused to be intimidated.

'Yes, I do.'

'I didn't realise you were a management consultant as well as a PA.'

Tess set her teeth at his sarcasm. 'You asked,' she reminded him with a defiant look. It wouldn't do Gabriel any harm at all to realise how much everyone at SpaceWorks disliked him.

And after waking up in his arms this morning, it wouldn't do her any harm to remember, either.

'Well, if you've quite finished your analysis, perhaps we can get on,' said Gabriel tightly, ignoring the fact that he had started the conversation. Stalking over to the printer, he picked up the finished pages and headed for his office.

'Finish those alterations and then you can start making up the final report. I'll be in my office. I don't want to be disturbed!'

He slammed the door shut behind him, leaving Tess staring after him in impotent rage.

'I see our boss is being his usual charming self this morning,' said an amused voice behind her, and she turned to see Niles who worked in the marketing department, and who was an inveterate flirt and an even worse gossip. Few people took him seriously, but it was impossible not to like him.

Unlike some, thought Tess darkly, thinking of Gabriel.

'What can I do for you, Niles?' she asked, and he strolled into the office, clasping a hand dramatically to his chest.

'Stop breaking my heart, Tess, and say you'll marry me.'

'I'm afraid I can't help you with that one,' said Tess, who was used to this routine. She sat back at her computer and reached for the next file. 'Anything else?'

'You can tell me what's going on between you and Gabriel Stearne,' Niles suggested, perching on the edge of her desk. 'There are all sorts of rumours going around the office about you two coming in together this morning with a baby.'

Amused at the idea of Tess having a secret affair with Gabriel, he started to laugh, only to break off as he caught sight of Harry's pram, and he turned to stare at her. 'Don't tell me it's true!'

Tess sighed. 'It's a long story, Niles, but it's not what you're thinking.'

'You're not sleeping with the boss?'

Only the faintest tinge of colour betrayed Tess's confusion. 'Of course not.' she said sharply. 'Niles, I'm very busy. Did you want something or are you just here to gossip?'

'No, I'm here in my capacity as social secretary,' he said grandly. 'We've decided to do something different this year for our charity bash. The idea is to have a promises auction, in aid of the children's hospital. It's a great night, so we're hoping everyone will come.'

'How does it work?'

'Haven't you ever been to one before?' Niles settled more comfortably onto her desk. 'You promise to do something—say, babysit for an evening—and anyone who wants a babysitter will bid for you, and the money goes to charity instead. This time, we're going to have a raffle as well,' he added.

'Frankly, some of the things people have offered aren't likely to attract that many bids, so we thought we'd run it as a kind of lucky dip. You buy a ticket, and win whatever has been promised for that number. It was the only way we could think of to get rid of some of them, but it should be laugh.'

He paused and looked expectantly at Tess. 'So what are you going to promise?'

'Me?'

'Come on, Tess, you've got to set a good example. Lynette in accounts is promising to wash your car wearing only a bikini!'

Tess laughed. 'I'm sure there'll be some heavy bidding for that one!'

'That's what we're hoping. But I bet you could match it if you tried. It's all in a good cause, remember.'

'Well, I'm certainly not putting my bikini on in October, but I'll try and think of something,' she promised.

'Tess, where is—?' Gabriel came out of his room and stopped dead at the sight of Tess laughing with Niles, who was perched far too familiarly on her desk.

Niles slid off at the expression on his face. 'Good morning, sir,' he said.

'I wondered what all the noise was about.' Gabriel was looking boot-faced. 'Haven't you both got something better to do than sit there gossiping?'

Tess opened her mouth to protest, but Niles got in first.

'I'm here about the staff party in November,' he said. 'We're running a promises auction to raise money for charity, and Tess was just agreeing to take part.'

'Really?' said Gabriel discouragingly.

'We're hoping we can count on your support too, sir. It would be a boost for staff morale if you'd come along.'

Gabriel had opened his mouth to refuse when he caught Tess's eye, and shut it again. He didn't want another lecture on treating employees like her precious Steve had. 'I'll do my best,' he said grudgingly.

'That's great.' Niles decided to push his luck. 'And you'll make a promise for the auction?'

'Yes, yes,' said Gabriel testily, waving Niles aside. 'Put me down for anything. Tess, I can't find the Liechenstein file.'

'Thank you, sir.' Niles grinned at Tess and made a thumbs-up sign behind Gabriel's back as he slid out of the office.

A briskly competent nanny appeared at twelve. Gabriel gave her the key to his apartment and directions as to how to get there, and she took Harry away. She assured them that she knew exactly how to deal with him, but his wails of protest as she pushed him in his pram out to the lift seemed to linger accusingly in the office long after he had gone.

After less than three hours' sleep, Tess knew that she ought to have been grateful not to have to think about the baby any more, but the office seemed strangely empty without him, and she kept turning to look for him.

It was a very long day. The proposal was completed at five o'clock and couriered round to meet the five-thirty deadline. As soon as it had gone, Tess was overwhelmed with exhaustion, and she collapsed into her chair. Her eyes felt gritty and there was a tight band inside her head. She wanted nothing more than to go home, soak in a deep bath and go to bed. At least the next day was Saturday. She could have a lie in and catch up on her lost sleep.

Yawning, she filed all the papers they had been using, checked her e-mail for any urgent messages, and decided that as the clock now stood at five forty-five she could legitimately leave the office.

Gabriel came in from his office as she was switching off her computer. 'Are you going home?'

'There's nothing else, is there?'

'No,' he said, but he hesitated.

'Are you sure?'

'Of course I'm sure,' he said irritably. How could he tell her that he didn't want her to leave? That he didn't want to go back to his impersonal apartment alone, with only that terrifyingly competent nanny for company?

There was a pause. Tess fumbled with her coat, suddenly unable to find the sleeve opening, and in the end Gabriel held the coat for her so that she could slip her arm inside.

'Thank you for all your help today,' he said as if the words had been forced out of him.

A thank you from Gabriel Stearne! Tess knew that she ought to feel triumphant, but all she could think was that he was standing very close. When Steve had complimented her, it had been easy to respond, but she wasn't used to Gabriel being nice, and she didn't know what to say. It was easier when he was being unpleasant, in a way.

'That's all right,' she said awkwardly. 'I was just doing my job. It's what you pay me for.'

Conscious that she had sounded rather ungracious, she made a big deal of fastening the buttons of her coat as he stepped away from her. Fixing a bright smile to her face, she bent to pick up her bag. 'I'll see you on Monday, then.'

'Have a good weekend,' said Gabriel in a strangely colourless voice. 'Goodnight, Tess.'

'Goodnight, Mr Stearne.'

'For God's sake, Tess!' he burst out, suddenly furious with her.

How dared she be so cool and formal with him when he had kissed her skin, when he had buried his face in her hair, when his hand had traced the soft contours of her body? 'We slept together last night,' he said savagely. 'In the circumstances, I think you could call me Gabriel, don't you?'

He was pleased to see a faint hint of colour along her cheekbones at his reminder. So she hadn't forgotten completely.

'If that's what you'd prefer,' she said stiltedly after a moment.

'It is,' Gabriel snapped. There was no need for her to make it sound as if he was forcing her into an unwanted intimacy. She hadn't called Steve Mr Robinson, had she? No, it had been Steve this, Steve that, Steve's a very nice man!

'I'll see you on Monday,' he said curtly, turning on his heel.

Letting herself into her house after an even slower bus ride than usual, Tess was conscious of a feeling of anticlimax. It was inevitable after coping with an unexpected baby and a crucial deadline, she told herself. Nothing whatsoever to do with not seeing Gabriel until Monday.

She wished he hadn't reminded her about sleeping together. She had tried so hard to dismiss their awakening as unimportant, and there had been times during the day when Gabriel had been so difficult that it had been easy to tell herself that she had put the entire incident out of her mind.

And then he had helped her into her coat, and his hands had brushed against her shoulders and memories had come back in a rush of sensation. It was all very well to tell herself that she had been practically asleep, but she could still feel his lips moving over her skin, still feel his hands hard against her with disturbing clarity.

Tess shivered anew at the memory and shut the front door behind her with unnecessary emphasis.

The red light was blinking on the answer machine in the kitchen. Glad of the distraction, she listened to the two messages while she took off her coat.

'Tess, it's Bella. Why haven't you rung me? I'm dying to know how you got on with the baby and—more importantly—how you got on with Gabriel Stearne. You promised you'd tell me everything, remember?'

Tess grimaced at Bella's words. She might have promised, but she wouldn't be telling her friend *quite* everything, that was for sure. She could tell her about Harry and changing his nappy, but not about ending up in bed with Gabriel, and certainly not about waking up with him! She would ring Bella back tomorrow and give her some very edited highlights when she was feeling better able to cope with her friend's probing questions. Sometimes Bella knew her a little too well for comfort.

The second message was from Andrew.

'Hi, sis, it's me. Thanks for your e-mail. I hate to ask, but I was wondering when you'd be able to send the cheque you mentioned? The landlord's hassling us about the deposit, and I'm really short of cash at the moment. I had a quote to repair the car after those joyriders pranged it too, and it's going to cost a packet.'

Tess hung up her coat with a sigh. She had been so proud when Andrew had got into university, but she'd had no idea how expensive his studies would prove to be. Not that he seemed to do much studying. From all she could gather, he spent most of his time playing sport or going out with friends.

He had got himself a part-time job in a pub to earn some extra cash so that he didn't have to rely on her too much, but she didn't want him working any more hours than he already did. He spent little enough time at his books as it was. She would just have to find the money from somewhere. Double or not, the overtime she had earned last night obviously wasn't going to be enough.

Too tired to think about it then, Tess wearily climbed the stairs to the bathroom and ran a hot bath. She felt better after a long, luxurious soak by candlelight. Her tense muscles had relaxed and her skin was pink and glowing by the time she got out. Wrapping herself in a towelling robe, she wandered downstairs to the kitchen in search of something to eat. She was rubbing her wet hair absently and contemplating the contents of her fridge without enthusiasm when the doorbell rang.

Tess frowned as she looked at her watch. Nine-thirty. Who would be calling now? One of her neighbours? She hoped it wasn't the man from number seventeen, who was the local Neighbourhood Watch contact and took his duties very seriously. He was always popping round at odd times, extolling the benefits of security lights and double locks.

Barefoot, she padded along the narrow hallway and peered cautiously through the peephole in the front door.

Her heart jolted when she saw who was standing on her step, and her hands weren't quite steady as she opened the door.

'Can we come in? Gabriel asked. He was holding a sleeping Harry in his arms, and he sounded oddly hesitant.

Without a word, Tess stood back to let him past into the narrow hall. 'What's the matter?' she said, oddly breathless as she closed the door behind them. 'Where's the nanny?'

'Gone.'

'Gone? Gone where?' Tess began, only to break off. Gabriel was looking so frayed that it seemed unfair to subject him to a cross-examination in the cramped and uncomfortable confines of her hall. 'You'd better come and sit down,' she said instead, pointing him towards the sitting room.

Gabriel lowered himself gratefully onto a small sofa facing the fireplace, and dropped his car keys onto the low wooden table in front of it. Harry was sound asleep. He shifted the baby carefully in his arms and wondered how he was going to explain to Tess why he had invaded her house and her private time once more.

His massive presence seemed to fill the room. Very conscious of her wet, tangled hair and pink face, Tess sat on the edge of an armchair and folded the towelling robe primly around her bare legs.

'I think you should tell me exactly what's happened,' she said, trying to sound as crisp as she could when she was half naked and her hair was dripping down her neck. She squeezed the ends with the towel. 'Couldn't the nanny find your apartment?'

'Oh, she found it all right, but apparently it's not what she's used to.' In spite of his uncharacteristically tired appearance, there was plenty of the old bite in Gabriel's voice as he recalled his reception when he had walked into the apartment. 'She insists on her own room and her own bathroom,' he went on, mimicking the girl's demands. 'She expects the use of a car, and regular time off. Oh, and meals provided. Sending her off to an apartment with an empty fridge was completely unacceptable!'

'Oh, dear,' said Tess weakly. 'Perhaps we should have taken the time to tell her what to expect.'

She hadn't been told what to expect last night, but she had coped, thought Gabriel. She hadn't made a fuss or irritated him with truculent demands. She hadn't complained about having to sleep in his bed or make do with take-away pizza.

He looked across at where she was perched on an armchair, and realised for the first time that she must have just stepped out of the bath. Her skin was glowing, and her hair hung damply around her face, and he had a sudden, sharp awareness that beneath the towelling robe she must be naked.

He forced his gaze back to the fire. 'When I got back to the apartment, it was to find Harry bawling and the so-called nanny more concerned about clarifying the terms of her contract than looking after the baby.'

Tess grimaced, imagining the scene. Gabriel's temper was short at the best of times, and after a broken night and a long, stressful day in the office he would have been in no mood to deal with hectoring demands.

'The final straw was when she refused to allow me to spend the night in my own apartment,' Gabriel went on grimly. 'She didn't like the fact that there was no bedroom door, and she clearly didn't trust me to stay on the couch.' He snorted at the memory. 'I told her I didn't anticipate any problems in keeping my hands off her, but that just caused more offence!

'I lost my temper in the end,' he confessed, and Tess was only surprised that he had kept it as long as he had. 'I told her that if she didn't like it she could go,' he said, deciding to omit the fact that he had put it in much stronger terms than that. 'I said I could look after Harry by myself.'

'And she took you at your word?'

'Yes.' Gabriel avoided her clear brown gaze. 'I know I shouldn't have snapped at her,' he said grudgingly, 'but I was tired and Harry was crying, and she wouldn't shut up. I thought I'd be able to manage without her...'

'But?' said Tess, resigned, when he trailed off.

'But I couldn't,' he admitted.

CHAPTER FIVE

'I DID try,' he said defensively. 'I changed his nappy and walked him around, the way we did last night, but he wouldn't stop crying, and when I gave him something to eat, he went purple and started choking. I was desperate in the end. I didn't know what to do.' He looked at Tess. 'All I could think of was you.'

There was a slight frown in his eyes as he remembered that humiliating sense of inadequacy and how instinctively he had thought of Tess: Tess with her cool voice and her cool air, Tess with her warm eyes and her warm body; Tess who was calm and competent and who wouldn't let him down.

'I couldn't ask Fionnula,' he went on, as if he needed to justify why he had turned to her. 'She's working tonight, some programme that's going out live, and anyway, she's still angry with me about standing her up last night. I couldn't think of anything else to do. I put Harry in the car and came over and…well, here we are.'

He looked down at the sleeping baby in his arms with an expression of baffled frustration. There was no trace now of the screaming bundle of furious energy he had been only half an hour ago. What could be so difficult about looking after a peacefully slumbering baby like this?

'He fell asleep in the car,' he told Tess, remembered relief at the sudden silence mingling with annoyance that Harry was making it so difficult to convince Tess of what he had been like. 'But I can't drive around all night.'

Tess was rubbing her hair with the towel, as if she needed something to do with her hands to disguise her uncertainty about the whole situation. She looked wary, thought Gabriel. She knew what he was going to ask her.

'Please, Tess,' he said, reflecting that he seemed to spend most of his time begging her to help him these days. 'I know it's a lot to ask. I know you didn't get much sleep last night, and how hard you've worked all day, but I really need you.'

He stopped, hearing too late what he had said. Tess had paused, one hand clutching the towel against her head, and it seemed to Gabriel that his words echoed mockingly in the sudden silence. *I really need you...need you...need you...*

'Well, you know,' he amended awkwardly.

Tess smiled a little crookedly as she lowered the towel. 'I know,' she said without meeting his eyes.

It was chastening to have to admit how useless he felt, but Gabriel set his teeth and floundered on. 'You must remember what it was like last night. Harry won't stay sleeping like this. He'll wake up and he'll cry and I won't know what to do with him. If you would just come back with me again tonight, I promise I'll make other arrangements tomorrow.'

He paused and looked at Tess, who was dabbing absently at the drips down her neck and avoiding his eyes. She was trying to think of a way to refuse, thought Gabriel with a sinking feeling.

'I'll give you anything you want if you'll come with me.' he said rashly.

She looked up at that. 'Anything?'

'Money...time off in lieu...a plane ticket to wherever you want...anything.'

'How about you promising to be nice to your staff for a change?'

Tess's voice was very dry. She hadn't meant it seriously, but Gabriel had said 'OK' almost before she had finished speaking, and she put her head on one side, considering how she might turn his dilemma into a general advantage.

'You'll acknowledge greetings instead of ignoring people the way you usually do?'

'Yes.'

'You'll say please and thank you?'

'Yes.'

'You'll come to the office party?'

Gabriel set his jaw. 'Yes.'

She lifted her brows in exaggerated surprise. 'You must be desperate.' she said.

'I am.'

The grey eyes looked directly into hers, and Tess saw with a trace of compunction that there were dark circles beneath them. His face was drawn and he needed a shave. She had been working hard in the run up to submitting the bid today, but Gabriel had worked even harder and longer. He had had no more sleep than she'd had last night, and after a frantic day in the office he hadn't even had the luxury of a long, hot bath nor any time to himself at all before being faced with a stroppy nanny and a screaming baby. No wonder he looked tired.

'All right,' she said abruptly.

She got to her feet before she had a chance to change her mind, inadvertently revealing a length of thigh as her robe slipped apart. Pulling it hastily together, she tightened the belt with unnecessary emphasis. 'You'll have to wait while I dry my hair and get dressed.'

'Of course,' said Gabriel with a smile.

His smile held nothing but a kind of weary relief, but Tess felt her heart stumble. He might not be smiling the way he had smiled at Harry, but he was smiling at *her*. She could hear the clock on the mantelpiece ticking into the silence, and she was suddenly, disturbingly aware of him, of his dark hair and his pale eyes, of the lines bracketing his mouth and the stubble on his jaw, of his hand cupping Harry against his chest.

She swallowed. 'Well…make yourself comfortable,' she said, and was horrified to hear that it came out as a croak rather than the gracious and composed invitation she had intended. 'I won't be long.'

'Tess?' said Gabriel abruptly as she turned to leave.

She paused with one hand on the door, and looked over her shoulder. 'Yes?'

'Thanks,' he said simply.

Upstairs, Tess tipped her head down and turned the hairdryer on full blast. She felt ridiculously thrown by Gabriel's smile. Really, she thought, she must be getting soft! She should have said no. She could have made up some excuse. Why hadn't she said that she was going out, or expecting an important phone call? Now Gabriel would expect her to give up all her free time whenever he needed her to help him out of his personal mess.

It wasn't as if he had ever done anything for her. She didn't even *like* the man! There was no reason for her to face another sleepless night when her body was already buzzing with exhaustion.

Except that he had thanked her.

Except that he had smiled.

Except that he had looked straight into her eyes and had said that he needed her.

Left alone in the sitting room, Gabriel let out a long sigh and settled himself back on the couch. As if sensing the tension draining out of him, Harry snuffled and snuggled closer.

'Make yourself comfortable,' Tess had said. Gabriel eased off his shoes and stretched out until he lay diagonally across the couch with his feet propped up on the coffee table, and Harry sprawled face down on his chest.

He could hear Tess moving around upstairs. It was a comforting sort of noise, and gradually Gabriel let himself relax. His gaze travelled around the room, taking it in for the first time. It was decorated in warm, rich colours, and the haphazard piles of books and objects that covered every surface gave the room a feel of cosy chaos.

Remembering how organised Tess was in the office, and the uncluttered efficiency of her desk, Gabriel lifted his brows in surprise. This wasn't the kind of room he had imagined her to come home to every night. It was somehow unexpected.

Like Tess.

The warmth and tranquillity of the room were having their effect. Gabriel tried to keep himself awake by studying the collection of unusual objects Tess had displayed in the alcoves on either side of the pretty Victorian fireplace. There was an old spice box and an ornate, oriental birdcage next to a photograph of a smiling couple in a heavy silver frame. Gabriel couldn't see it clearly from where he was, and it would have disturbed Harry if he had got up to inspect the picture. He had better stay right where he was.

From upstairs came the sound of a hair-dryer. She would be down in a minute, and he could have a closer look at the photo then. In the meantime, there would be no harm in closing his eyes for a minute…

Tess's hair had dried into a wayward cloud. Unable to control it any other way, she tied it back with a scrunchie and surveyed her reflection critically. In jeans and a sweatshirt, she looked practical rather than pretty, she decided. Safe rather than seductive. Not like a girl who would invite her boss to bed, or open the door to him wearing only a towelling robe.

And what exactly do you need to feel safe about? Tess asked herself, but couldn't come up with a satisfactory answer. She concentrated on packing her bag instead, scrabbling through her drawers to find a more demure nightdress this time, just in case she ended up sharing a bed with Gabriel again.

A slow shiver snaked down her spine at the memory of waking that morning with his arms around her, and his body hard against her own. No, it would be safer if she dealt with Harry herself tonight, and let Gabriel sleep on the sofa.

Safer. There was that word again.

Zipping up her bag with unnecessary emphasis, Tess carried it downstairs and dropped it by the front door.

She hesitated outside the sitting room. It was ridiculous to be nervous at the thought of spending another night with him. It wasn't as if it were a date. It was just a practical arrangement. Gabriel was her boss and, if it wasn't for Harry, there was no way he would be sitting on her sofa, waiting to drive her back to his apartment. He would be out with the likes of Fionnula Jenkins and his PA would be the very last person on his mind.

So why was her heart thudding at the thought of the night ahead?

Taking a deep breath, Tess pushed open the door. 'I'm rea—' she began, only to break off as she saw Gabriel sprawled across the sofa, Harry spread-eagled on his chest.

Both were sound asleep.

She stood and looked down at them for a moment, a curious expression in her eyes. In sleep, the harsh lines of Gabriel's face had softened, and he had lost that grim, guarded look that was so typical of him. His head had fallen to one side, and the dark hair flopped over his forehead in a way that he would hate if he were awake. Tess's fingers twitched with an involuntary impulse to smooth it back into place.

Abruptly, she stepped back out of reach.

If she had any sense, she told herself severely, she would shake Gabriel awake and make him drive her back to his cold, characterless apartment. This was her home. He had no business falling asleep here.

But he had looked so tired, and she didn't have the heart to wake either of them.

Gabriel's car keys were sitting on the coffee table. Tess picked them up and weighed them in her hand for a moment's indecision before making up her mind. She let herself quietly out of the house and found the car parked almost right outside. Trust Gabriel to get the best spot.

As she had hoped, he had brought Harry in the carry-cot which he had detached from the pram. A bottle and a spare nappy were on the seat beside it. He had obviously set out prepared for the worst. Tess put them in the cot and carried them all back inside.

Neither Gabriel nor Harry had stirred. Very gently, Tess lifted the baby off Gabriel's chest. He squirmed and mouthed in instinctive protest at being moved from his comfortable position, but he didn't wake, and she was able to carry him upstairs and lay him in his cot beside her bed.

There was a duvet on Andrew's bed. Bundling it up, she took it downstairs and covered Gabriel as best she could. The wayward lock of hair was still straggling over his forehead. Succumbing to temptation, Tess pushed it gently away from his face. Her fingers lingered for a moment against his temple before she realised what she was doing and snatched her hand away. A faint flush stained her cheeks as she left him, switching off the light with a sharp click as she went.

Gabriel woke with a stiff neck and an even stiffer back. He was lying half on, half off a couch that was several feet too short for him, and his face was pressed uncomfortably into a cushion.

He sat up with a groan, disentangling himself with difficulty from a mass of bedding. Where had all that come from? he wondered blearily.

Dropping his head into his hands, he raked his fingers through his hair. He remembered arriving at Tess's house, and how she had looked when she'd opened the door with her face pink and glowing and her hair all damp and tangled. He remembered the sense of relief when she'd agreed to come with him, leaning back on the couch as the iron bands of tension that had held him in their grip had loosened and unlocked one by one.

And then...nothing. He must have fallen asleep.

Gabriel looked at his watch and grimaced as he got stiffly to his feet. He had slept the night through!

Cautiously, he opened the sitting room door. A radio was playing somewhere, and he followed the sound down the narrow hallway, past the wooden stairs, and into a surprisingly large kitchen. Autumn sun poured through the French windows, which opened onto a tiny patio garden, and made him blink after the dimness of the hall.

Tess was sitting at a scrubbed pine table, giving Harry a bottle of milk. She looked up as Gabriel appeared in the doorway. 'Good morning,' she said.

'Sorry,' he said, rubbing a hand over his face. 'I didn't mean to fall asleep.'

'You were tired.'

She did her best to sound casual, as if she hadn't even noticed the intimacy of his rumpled clothes and dark, dishevelled hair. There was a red mark across his cheek where his face had been pressed into the braid of one of the cushions.

'I must have been to have slept like that.' Gabriel sat down at the table, wincing at the stiffness of his muscles. 'Thanks for tucking me up,' he added.

There was an odd note in his voice, and a hint of colour stole into Tess's cheeks. What if he had been aware of her tenderly smoothing the hair from his forehead? Her fingertips prickled with the remembered feel of stubble on his warm skin. 'I didn't want you to get cold,' she said, avoiding his eyes.

A pause.

'How was Harry last night?' asked Gabriel after a moment.

'He woke up a couple of times, but the second time I took him into bed with me, and after that he was fine.'

As well he might have been, Gabriel thought involuntarily. He remembered what it was like being in bed with Tess himself.

'You should have woken me,' he said stiffly, uncomfortably aware of the awkwardness of the situation. How the hell were you supposed to behave to your PA when you had fallen asleep on her? 'I didn't mean you to cope with him by yourself.'

'It was no problem.'

Typical Tess, thought Gabriel with an edge of resentment. Nothing was ever a problem for her.

He studied her as she sat Harry up and rubbed his back. There was a confidence about the way she dealt with the baby now. It was hard to believe that she had once been as nervous about Harry as he still was. There must be some kind of mysterious feminine gene that gave her the assurance he lacked.

She was wearing a blue sweatshirt, the sleeves pushed casually above her delicate wrists, and the sunlight through the window brought out the gold in her hair. This morning, she had tied it back in a loose plait, which made her look younger and much more relaxed than she did in the office, but there was still a coolness and a freshness about her that was characteristic.

Her neatness was a reproach. Conscious suddenly of his own crumpled state, Gabriel rubbed a palm over his jaw with a grimace.

'Why don't you have a shower?' Tess suggested. 'You'd feel better. There's a razor in the bathroom, too, if you wanted to shave. You can't miss the bathroom—it's right at the top of the stairs.'

Whose razor was it? Gabriel wondered as he climbed the wooden stairs with their ridiculously narrow steps.

As Tess had predicted, he found the bathroom without difficulty, but she hadn't warned him about the array of frivolous, luxurious silk lingerie drying on a cord strung over the bathtub. Raising his eyebrows, Gabriel moved it cautiously out of the way. He wished he hadn't seen it. It was proving hard enough to keep his image of Tess as a cool, professional secretary intact as it was without knowing that beneath those prim grey suits of hers she was wearing *that*.

The razor proved to be of an old-fashioned variety, but he managed a shave, only cutting himself twice, and by the time he had showered he realised that Tess had been right: he did feel better.

The smell of freshly brewed coffee wafted up the stairs. Gabriel sniffed appreciatively as he went back into the kitchen. 'That smells good.'

Tess turned quickly from where she was trying to plunge the cafetière one-handed, with Harry on her hip.

'Here, let me,' said Gabriel.

She stepped away, very aware of his strong hands, and the dark hair still wet from the shower and sleeked close to his head.

'Um...I'm sorry about all the washing,' she said, embarrassed. 'I forgot all about it.'

'No problem,' said Gabriel briefly, his eyes on the cafetière. 'I moved it so it didn't get wet, but I've put it back.'

A queer feeling stirred inside Tess at the thought of his hands on her underwear. 'Thanks.' She cleared her throat. 'Well...how about a coffee?' Shifting Harry onto her other hip, she got two mugs out of the cupboard above.

'You're getting good at this,' commented Gabriel, nodding at Harry, who was drooling placidly onto her sweatshirt, and looking quite at home on her hip.

'I know.' Relieved at the change of subject, Tess ra her fingers through Harry's downy curls. 'I was terrifie of him when he first arrived, but I'm getting quite fond him now,' she confessed.

'I need to do something about tracking down h mother.' Gabriel poured coffee into the mugs and carrie them over to the table. 'There wasn't time yesterday b finding her is a priority now. I'll get private investigato onto it.'

He sat down and frowned into his coffee as he ponderé who best to approach. He presumed that there would I people in London who could do the job, but if Leanne ha indeed gone back to the Caribbean, it might be better go through a firm in the States. 'It can't take that long find her, surely,' he said.

'I would have thought it would be a few days at leasi said Tess, who was also considering the matter. 'And one you've found her, you've still got to get her back here. think we should plan on having him for a week.'

'A week!' Gabriel knew that she was right, but it didr make him like the situation any better. He sighed. 'I have to try and get hold of another nanny, but there's st the problem of my apartment. I don't fancy another who week of sleeping on the couch! Perhaps I should book in a hotel?' he added as the thought occurred to him. 'I cou get a separate room for the nanny and Harry.'

'That seems a bit extravagant,' commented Tes blowing on her coffee to cool it.

'Have you got any better ideas?'

This was the opening she had been waiting for. 'Yes she said with a level look. 'I could carry on helping yo to look after him.'

'*You*? I thought you didn't know anything about b bies?'

'I'm learning fast.' Tess hesitated. 'Look, Harry's ju settling down. Why disrupt him again just when he's ge ting used to us? He's been passed around enough recently as it is.'

There were definite advantages to the idea, Gabriel had to admit. Not the least of which was the time it would save in trying to find a nanny who would stay in his apartment. Even if he found one prepared to put up with the lack of doors, the chances were that she wouldn't last long. As Tess had pointed out so succinctly, his management style wasn't the easiest.

But it didn't add up. Gabriel regarded her suspiciously, his dark brows drawn together in a frown and the pale grey eyes uncomfortably keen. 'Why would you want to give up your weekend, not to mention an entire week, looking after a baby who has nothing to do with you and is, if anybody's, my responsibility?'

Tess fidgeted with her mug. 'I'm not suggesting I do it for free,' she said, and made herself look straight at him. 'I'd expect to be paid on top of my salary.'

Ah, so that was it. Money. He might have guessed, thought Gabriel cynically. 'You want money?'

Tess flushed slightly at his tone. 'I don't think it's unreasonable,' she said, putting up her chin. 'I'd be giving up all my free time for a weekend and, as we've discovered, looking after a baby is hard work.'

'I don't deny it.'

Gabriel wasn't sure why he felt disillusioned. He had always known that money was the greatest motivator of them all. He just hadn't had Tess down as a materialist. He should have known better. In his experience, women talked a lot about emotions but, when it came down to it, he had yet to meet one whose motives weren't entirely mercenary at heart, no matter how hard she tried to dress them up in woolly sentiment. Why had he expected Tess to be any different?

'I'm sure we could come to some arrangement,' he said

distantly. 'But what about your job? I need someone to look after Harry, but I also need you in the office.'

'I could take him in with me,' said Tess, trying not to sound too eager. 'Things should be quieter next week and, if it does get busy, I could always ask one of the other secretaries to help me out. I think it could work.'

Why was she so keen to take on the job? Gabriel wondered, and then took himself to task. What was it to him if Tess was prepared to do anything for money? She was saving him the trouble of finding someone else to help him look after Harry, and that was all that mattered.

'All right,' he said briskly. 'If you think that you can manage, we'll carry on as we are.'

Tess was relieved. She had worked out on the back of an envelope earlier that morning how much overtime she could earn, and if she included nights—and she didn't see why she shouldn't—it came to a surprisingly large sum. It would be hard work, of course, but it was only for a week, and at the end of it she would be able to send Andrew enough to pay off most of his outstanding debts.

She saw Gabriel pushing back his chair as if making ready to leave and she bit her lip. 'There is just one thing,' she said. 'Would you mind staying here?'

Gabriel sank slowly back into his chair. 'Wouldn't *you* mind?' he countered. 'You've always struck me as someone who keeps her private and her professional life quite separate.'

'I do usually,' she said, 'but I don't really want to spend the next week in your apartment. It's not very suitable for a baby,' she excused herself. 'And at least here I've got a spare room. You wouldn't have to sleep on the sofa again.'

'That would make a nice change,' he conceded dryly. He looked directly at Tess. 'Are you sure?'

Tess took a sharp breath. 'Yes, I'm sure.'

'In that case, I'll go home and get some clean clothes. I can bring the rest of Harry's stuff back with me. And then,' said Gabriel, getting to his feet, 'I think we're going to have to go shopping.'

Inevitably, it was awkward at first. There was something uncomfortably intimate about going to the supermarket with Gabriel, finding out what vegetables he liked, puzzling over the array of different nappies on sale, standing next to him in the checkout queue.

Did they look as out of place as they felt? Tess wondered. Or would anyone walking past them as they regarded the baby goods assume that they were an ordinary couple, with their first baby gurgling happily in the trolley beside them?

Her eyes slid sideways to Gabriel who was reading the instructions on the back of a packet of rusks with a sceptical expression. No, he might be a lot of things, but ordinary would never be one of them. In spite of his unexceptional jeans and dark blue guernsey, there was a toughness about him that marked him out in this prosaic setting.

Tess had to keep reminding herself that this was just a job, and that Gabriel was just her boss—and a difficult, exacting boss at that! But it was hard to keep up the formality when Gabriel, evidently deciding that the only thing to do was to throw money at the problem, swept her off to a store and insisted on buying an entire range of equipment for Harry.

'We can't keep using that old pram,' he said roughly. 'I'm sick of taking it to pieces and putting it together again. I'm going to buy him a proper cot, and his mother can have it—if she ever reappears!'

He got hold of an assistant who could hardly believe her luck when she realised that they needed help and that money was no object. It wasn't long before they found themselves loading Gabriel's car with a high chair, a cot with bedding, a special mat for Harry, an assortment of bibs, bowls and bottles, and a bouncy chair that the assistant had assured them that he would enjoy. Tess had found some little outfits, too, that had gone in with it all, along with some educational toys that the assistant had recommended, although they'd had more fun choosing a glove puppet and arguing over the merits of a mischievous fox and a dopey-looking rabbit.

Fun. It seemed an odd word to associate with the dour Gabriel, thought Tess as they drove back to her house but, once the initial constraint had evaporated, he had been surprisingly easy to get on with.

She slid a puzzled glance at him, her gaze lingering on the forceful planes and angles of his face and coming to rest at last on his stern mouth. It looked cool and firm, but those lips had been warm against her throat…

Tess jerked her eyes away. Her heart was drumming with unwanted memories and she had to take a steadying breath. She was supposed to have forgotten how he had kissed her.

She *had* forgotten, Tess tried to convince herself. It was just that every now and then the memory would catch her unawares, and she would have to forget it all over again.

Harry was hungry by the time they got home. Gabriel took a turn at feeding him while Tess heated some soup for lunch, and he studied her covertly as she stood with her back to him at the stove, stirring. Funny how he had never realised before what a good figure she had. Nor how her face lit when she smiled.

Gabriel forced himself to look away. He stared instead at the photographs, postcards and cartoons pinned to a board by the table. In pride of place was an enlargement of a good-looking young man leaning proudly against the bonnet of a car. His arms were folded, and his face was split by a broad grin.

A boyfriend? Gabriel frowned. The boy in the photograph looked much younger than Tess, but that didn't mean very much.

'Who's that?' The question came out more abruptly than he intended.

Tess turned to see what he was looking at. Cupping her hand beneath the wooden spoon to catch any drips, she came over to follow his gaze. 'Oh, that's Andrew,' she said.

'Andrew?' Even to his own ears, Gabriel sounded hostile, and Tess glanced at him curiously.

'My brother,' she explained. 'I took that picture of him on his twenty-first earlier this year.' She shook her head at the photograph, but she was smiling. 'He loves that old car.'

She didn't add that she had given him most of the money to buy it. It had been little more than a heap of metal then, so heaven knew what kind of state it was in now that the joyriders had finished with it.

Standing beside Gabriel's chair, she was close enough for him to smell her perfume. Looking up at her, he could see how her expression softened as she thought about her brother. The corner of her mouth curved upwards in a fond smile, and Gabriel was conscious of a pang of something that he might have suspected was jealousy if he hadn't known better.

Because how could he possibly be jealous?

He looked back down at Harry. 'I didn't know you had a brother,' he said, and it occurred to him that there were an awful lot of things about Tess that he didn't know.

Tess went back to her soup. 'There's just the two of us,' she told him. 'My parents were killed in an accident, twelve years ago now. Andrew was only nine, and I've looked after him ever since.' She stirred, remembering. 'He was just a little boy. It was terrible for him.'

Gabriel thought that it must have been terrible for her too, losing both her parents and finding herself responsible for a small boy. He frowned. 'You can't have been very old yourself,' he said.

'I was twenty-two. My parents moved down from Edinburgh for Dad's job not long before the accident. They'd bought this house, so at least Andrew and I had somewhere to live, but Dad was never very good with money, and there was hardly anything else. I'd just finished a secretarial course and I'd wanted to travel, but Andrew was still at primary school, so I took the first job I was offered.'

'With Steve Robinson?'

'No, I had another job before that.' There was a certain reserve in Tess's voice and she frowned down at the soup she was mindlessly stirring. She tried not to think too much about that job and how it had ended. More than ten years ago now, but the memory of her humiliation still hurt.

'When I left there, I temped for a while, but it was difficult with Andrew at school. Then I went to SpaceWorks for a two week assignment, and I've been there ever since.

'Steve was fantastic,' she remembered gratefully. 'He believes that businesses should be flexible, and make allowances for the fact that their employees have to juggle their commitments at work and at home. So it was never a problem if I had to go home early to pick Andrew up from school or stay with him if he was sick.'

Gabriel set the empty bottle carefully on the table and sat Harry up to pat his back. 'No wonder you're so loyal to Steve Robinson,' he said, conscious of the same pinch of jealousy he had felt when she'd talked about her brother. Except that it *wasn't* jealousy, of course.

'It's not just me,' said Tess, on the defensive for some reason. 'Steve was like that with everybody. Working for him wasn't like a job. It was like being part of a family, until—'

'Until I came along?'

There was a pause, while they both remembered belatedly that they weren't two friends talking. He was her boss, and she was his PA.

'Yes,' she said. 'Until then.'

Only the day before yesterday they had disliked each other intensely, she remembered. And today?

Today, Tess wasn't sure. The realisation left her edgy and unsettled. It wasn't that she had changed her mind, nor that she suddenly liked Gabriel.

But perhaps she didn't dislike him quite as much as she had thought.

CHAPTER SIX

'THINGS are easier now, of course,' she said, making an effort to steer the conversation away from what felt like dangerous ground. 'Andrew's away at university, so I don't need to make time for him any more, just money.'

Tess smiled wryly as she poured the soup into two bowls. 'He's just started his final year. Sometimes I wonder how he's got as far as he has.' She sighed. 'He never seems to do any work. He just has a good time.

'I was so pleased when he got into university,' she confided, setting the bowls on the table and turning to find some spoons, 'but I had no idea how expensive it was going to be.

'I know it's hard for students nowadays, but Andrew always seems to be in debt. He still owes money from last year, and now he and some friends are trying to rent a house, but the landlord is demanding a huge deposit which none of them can afford. He's lost his car, too. Some boys took it for a joyride, and according to Andrew they've practically written it off. It's going to cost a fortune to repair.'

Sighing, Tess sat down at the table, only to get up again as she remembered the bread. 'That's why I was so keen to earn some extra money looking after Harry,' she told Gabriel, who was struggling to slot the baby into his new bouncy chair.

He looked up, the light grey eyes suddenly alert. 'Oh?' he said.

'I'd thought about asking you for a raise,' she confessed, 'but I know it's a generous salary as it is, and, anyway, it would soon get swallowed up just by the expense of living

NO POSTAGE
NECESSARY
IF MAILED
IN THE
UNITED STATES

BUSINESS REPLY MAIL
FIRST-CLASS MAIL   PERMIT NO. 717-003   BUFFALO, NY

POSTAGE WILL BE PAID BY ADDRESSEE

HARLEQUIN READER SERVICE
3010 WALDEN AVE
PO BOX 1867
BUFFALO NY 14240-9952

Play The

Lucky Hearts Game

and get...

FREE BOOKS & a FREE GIFT...
YOURS to KEEP!

Yes! I have scratched off the silver card. Please send me my **2 FREE BOOKS** and **FREE GIFT**. I understand that I am under no obligation to purchase any books as explained on the back of this card.

Scratch Here!
then look below to see what your cards get you...

DETACH AND MAIL CARD TODAY! (H-R-02/02)

386 HDL DH3Q   **186 HDL DH3P**

NAME   (PLEASE PRINT CLEARLY)

ADDRESS

APT.#   CITY

STATE/PROV.   ZIP/POSTAL CODE

Twenty-one gets you
2 FREE BOOKS and
a **FREE GIFT!**

Twenty gets you
2 FREE BOOKS!

Nineteen gets you
1 FREE BOOK!

TRY AGAIN!

Offer limited to one per household and not valid to current Harlequin Romance® subscribers. All orders subject to approval.

Visit us online at
www.eHarlequin.com

in London. I worked out that overtime for a week would give me a lump sum which I could send to Andrew so that he could sort out his accommodation and get his car fixed. I'd like him to give up his pub job, too. He needs to spend more time studying—it's not that long until his finals.'

She trailed off as she noticed that Gabriel was looking at her with a most peculiar expression. Tess couldn't decipher it at all, but she had a nasty feeling that she had just convinced him that she was obsessed by money.

Why had she told him all that about Andrew? Tess agonised. It wasn't like her to pour out her problems to anyone, least of all Gabriel Stearne. He wasn't interested in her petty little worries.

'Well, anyway, that's why I'm happy to spend this week looking after Harry,' she said awkwardly. 'I'm afraid my motives are entirely mercenary,' she went on in a flip voice to disguise her embarrassment. 'But, then, you probably guessed that.'

'Yes, I did,' said Gabriel slowly, 'but I didn't know why you needed the money.' He was disconcerted by the lightening of his heart. There shouldn't be any reason why it made a difference knowing that Tess hadn't wanted the money for herself, but somehow it did.

'I understand that you want to help your brother,' he said almost roughly, 'but you can't keep paying his debts for him. You said that he's twenty-one? Isn't it about time he learned that he has to stand on his own two feet?'

'I know,' said Tess, to whom this was a familiar dilemma. 'I feel responsible for him, though. I'm sure my parents would have helped him out. And anyway,' she went on, plucking up spirit, 'you're one to talk! You've taken on responsibility for your brother's baby.'

'Only temporarily,' Gabriel began to object, before acknowledging her point with a rather twisted smile. 'I guess I do feel responsible for Greg,' he admitted. 'I grew up in London, did you know that?'

'No, no, I didn't,' said Tess, thrown by the apparent change of subject, but intrigued by the idea of Gabriel as a boy. A British background explained some of the things that had puzzled her about him, the way he spoke that didn't quite fit with his American accent, that air he had of not quite belonging on one side of the Atlantic nor the other.

'My father left when I was fourteen,' Gabriel told her. 'Traded in his old family for a new one—it happens all the time.'

He shrugged. 'My mother is American, and she took me back to the States. Ray Stearne had been the boy next door when she was growing up, and they picked up right where they'd left off. Going home was the best thing that ever happened to my mother.

'It can't have been very easy having a sullen adolescent around the whole time, but Ray was very good to me, and when they married, I took his name. He was certainly more of a father to me than mine ever was,' he added with a trace of bitterness. 'It was Ray who spent time with me when my mother was wrapped up with Greg, Ray who encouraged me to set up on my own and lent me money to start my first business. I feel I owe it to him to bail Greg out of trouble. Greg's the centre of their lives, and they would only be upset if they heard the half of what he gets up to.'

'He sounds so charming on the phone,' commented Tess, remembering Greg's warm, treacly voice.

'Sure, he's charming,' said Gabriel. 'That's part of the trouble. Everybody loves him, everybody makes allowances for him, everybody falls over themselves to help him out. It would probably do Greg good to do some work for a change but, between Ray and me, he's never needed to. Ray gives him a generous allowance and, when he's spent that, he gives me a call. He says one of us might as well enjoy my money.' Gabriel gave another shrug. 'Perhaps he's right.'

Tess eyed him covertly as she drank her soup. For such a demanding and intolerant man, he seemed oddly resigned to his feckless brother's activities.

She had been strangely moved by Gabriel's terse account of his background. It wasn't, as he had said, that unusual a story, and in many ways he had been lucky in finding such a supportive stepfather, but still she had found herself aching for the boy he had been: abandoned by his father, uprooted from everything familiar and taken to a new country. No wonder he wore that guarded expression sometimes. Fourteen wasn't an easy age at the best of times.

Remembering how difficult Andrew had been then, Tess was half tempted to offer Gabriel sympathy, but something in his face told her it wouldn't be welcome. 'Have you had any news of your stepfather?' she asked him instead.

'I rang yesterday evening, after you'd gone home.' Gabriel seemed to welcome the change of subject. 'He'd had the operation, but was still in intensive care.' He glanced at his watch. 'I'll ring after lunch and see how he is today.'

'Are you going to go over and see him?'

'I'd planned to, but I can't leave Harry now.' There was a crease between Gabriel's dark brows as he looked down at the baby happily pulling at his feet in the bouncy chair. 'I'll have to track down his mother first and, as you pointed out earlier, that could take some time. If I can't, I guess we'll have to hope his grandmother reclaims him sooner or later, but there's no guarantee that she'll come back at all.'

He looked so concerned that Tess had an unaccountable impulse to reassure him. 'You'll find her,' she said. 'And, if your stepfather takes a turn for the worse, you can fly over in a few hours, and leave Harry with me. In fact, why not go anyway? I'm sure I could manage on my own if I had to.'

Tess could probably manage anything, thought Gabriel. 'I'm sure you could, but I hope that won't be necessary,' he said, unable to explain, even to himself, his reluctance to book a flight straight away. It wasn't as if he was any good at dealing with the baby. Why not go and see Ray as he had planned? Surely he didn't really want to stay with her and the baby in this small, cluttered, oddly comfortable house any longer than he had to?

Did he?

Of course he didn't.

After lunch, they put Harry to sleep in Tess's bedroom in his new cot. While Tess covered the mattress with a sheet and took the blanket out of its wrapping, Gabriel held the baby and looked around him, trying not to appear too obviously interested.

Yes, he could imagine Tess in here. It was a cool, light room with stripped floorboards and ethnic fabrics. The morning sun would stream through the windows and splash across the bed. He could imagine her all too clearly, in fact. He could practically see her lying there, stirring, stretching, opening her eyes with a sleepy smile, the way she had smiled when she had woken in his bed.

Throat very dry, Gabriel handed Harry over and took refuge in irritation. 'Why do none of your doors have any handles?' he demanded as they backed out of the room, leaving the door ajar. 'Every time I went to open one this morning, all I found was a hole.'

'They work all right,' said Tess defensively. 'Anyway, you can't complain. Your apartment hasn't even got any doors.'

'There's no point in having them at all if you can't shut them.'

'I don't need to shut them when I'm here on my own,' she pointed out as they made their way back down to the kitchen. 'Besides, they'll work fine when I've finished with them. Andrew stripped all the doors for me when he was home in the summer, and I bought some wonderful Victorian doorknobs in an antiques market. Look.' She took one down from the pile that had been gathering dust on top of the fridge to show him. 'Aren't they lovely?'

Gabriel inspected the mechanism. 'Very pretty,' he said with an ironic look, 'but not much use sitting on top of the fridge.'

'Andrew had to go back to university before he had a chance to put them on,' she explained. 'He promised he'd do them at Christmas.'

'But all you need is a screwdriver,' Gabriel objected, putting the doorknob back with the others. 'It would only take a few minutes.'

'I know, but I hate doing things like that,' she confessed in a burst of confidence. 'I'd rather do without doorknobs than tackle any kind of DIY.'

'You surprise me,' he said, regarding her thoughtfully. 'I'd have said you were a very practical person.'

'I'm organised. That's not the same as being practical. I'm hopeless when it comes to using my hands.'

She held them out with a rueful smile, as if to demonstrate their incompetence, and, quite without thinking, Gabriel took them and inspected them. They were beautifully shaped, with long, slender fingers and very clean, immaculately manicured nails.

Tess was right, he thought absently as he turned them over to rub his thumbs over her palms. They weren't practical hands at all. They were soft and smooth; they were warm. They were the same hands that had slid around his neck when they had woken up together in his apartment.

Gabriel dropped them abruptly.

'Have you got a screwdriver?'

'Wh-what?' Tess stared at him, dry-mouthed. She had been mesmerised by the feel of his fingers, the gentle stroke of his thumbs across her palms. He had hardly been touching her, probably hadn't even realised what he was doing, so why did it feel as if the graze of his skin against hers had been charged with an electricity that was still sparking and shorting along bones.

Swallowing, her eyes fell to her hands. She half expected to see scorches across her palms where they burned from his touch, but they just hung there at the ends of her arms, looking perfectly normal but feeling extremely odd, as if they didn't quite belong to her.

What did she normally do with her hands when she wasn't using them? Tess couldn't remember. She ended up folding her arms and tucking her hands away out of sight in an unconsciously defensive gesture.

'A what?' she said again, moistening her lips as she realised that Gabriel was still waiting for an answer.

'A screwdriver,' he repeated. 'If you've got one, I could put the door handles on for you.'

Tess's jaw dropped. The Gabriel Stearnes of this world weren't domesticated animals. They were like big cats, padding through the urban jungle, where home was just a place to sleep and survival of the fittest was all that mattered. They didn't do DIY.

'Why are you looking like that?' he said. 'How do you think I started out in construction business? I used to get my hands dirty the same as anyone else. I might spend all my time in the office now, but I can still tell a spanner from a screwdriver.'

'You mean you could really fit all these doorknobs for me?' said Tess doubtfully, still struggling to assimilate this new idea of Gabriel as man about the house.

'If you'd like me to.'

'Well, if you're sure it's no trouble...'

'It'll only take me five minutes.'

In the end he not only put handles on all the doors, but mended the dripping tap in the bathroom, changed an awkward light bulb on the landing that Tess had never been able to reach, oiled the hinges on a creaking cupboard door and fixed a mirror to the wall in her bedroom, a job which she had been meaning to do for over two years.

'What about that?' he said, coming into the kitchen where Tess was pottering around, and pointing at the shelf unit which was propped forlornly against the wall. 'Where do you want it to go?'

'There's no need for you to bother,' Tess began feebly, but Gabriel was already measuring the length of the shelf.

His movements were quick and economical, and she studied him under her lashes as she began preparing the meal for that night. She couldn't get used to him like this, with dust from the drill in his dark hair, and a dirty mark on his cheek, but at the same time it felt strangely comfortable to have him moving around her house.

It felt almost *right*.

'About here?'

Gabriel's voice broke into her thoughts and made her start. He was looking at her oddly, and a little colour stole into her cheeks. Had he noticed her staring at him?

'Yes, about there is fine, thanks,' she muttered, turning back to the onions she was chopping, but she could feel his eyes on her with a puzzled expression, and when the phone rang suddenly in the silence, she seized it quickly, grateful for the diversion.

She soon wished that she hadn't. It was Bella, wanting to know why Tess hadn't returned her call the evening before. 'Didn't you get my message?' she demanded.

'Yes, I did.' Tess turned her back on Gabriel and carried the cordless phone over to the French windows, as far away from him as she could get. 'I would have called you back but something came up,' she said awkwardly.

'What? Don't tell me you're still looking after that baby!'

'Well, sort of.'

'Tess, what's going on?'

Beginning to feel harassed, Tess lowered her voice. 'Nothing,' she said.

'Then why are you being so cagey? Have you got someone with you?' Bella's voice sharpened. 'Is it Gabriel Stearne?'

As Gabriel chose that moment to start drilling, it was difficult for Tess to claim, as she had intended, that she was on her own. Hastily, she opened the French windows and stepped into the garden, where she hoped she would be out of earshot.

'Look, it's perfectly simple,' she said, and gave Bella the bare outlines of the previous forty-eight hours, prudently keeping details like sharing Gabriel's bed to herself. She would never hear the end of it if Bella got wind of *that*.

'So, let me get this right,' said Bella when she had finished. 'You're spending the weekend with your boss, a man you said you hated. You're looking after his baby—'

'His brother's baby,' Tess put in feebly, but was ignored.

'For him; he spent all last night with you—'

'On my sofa—'

'And now he's putting up *shelves* for you?'

'It's not how it sounds,' said Tess, uncomfortably aware of how it *did* sound.

There was a pregnant pause.

'Tess,' said Bella sternly, 'you're not going to do anything stupid like fall in love with your boss, are you?'

'Fall in love with—?' Tess spluttered furiously. 'Of course I'm not! Don't be so ridiculous, Bella!'

Gabriel looked up as Tess stalked back into the kitchen, cutting the connection on the phone with unnecessary emphasis. Her cheeks were flaming and the golden-brown eyes were dangerously bright.

'You look very cross,' he commented. 'What's up?'

Tess slammed the phone back into its cradle. 'I am not in the least cross,' she said through gritted teeth, 'and nothing is *up*!'

But Bella's warning had done its work. The easy atmosphere of the afternoon had evaporated, leaving Tess excruciatingly aware of Gabriel. Had she really thought it was comfortable to have him in the house? Now his presence made her twitchy and unsettled, and she found herself avoiding his eyes and edging warily around him as they put Harry to bed, as if even an accidental contact would send an electric charge jolting through her.

She half hoped that the baby would prove difficult about going to sleep in his new cot, so that she would have something to do all evening but, perversely, Harry settled immediately. Tess looked at her watch in something like despair as she tiptoed out of the bedroom. Only quarter past seven. Still the whole evening to get through!

'I—er—I think I'll have a bath before supper,' she told Gabriel stiltedly.

Lying up to her neck in bubbles, Tess sipped her drink and tried to relax by focusing on the flickering flames of the candles she had placed at the end of the bath, but Bella's words kept sneaking into her mind.

You're not going to do anything stupid like fall in love with your boss, are you?

Of course, the suggestion was absolutely ridiculous. There was no question of her falling in love with Gabriel. Once before, she had got involved with someone at work, and it had ended in disaster. There was no way she was going to repeat that particular mistake.

And anyway, she didn't even like Gabriel—at least, not much. The very idea was laughable.

By the time she had dried herself and dressed in the dowdiest and least seductive clothes she could find, Tess had talked herself into a mood of brittle bravery. She was not—repeat *not*—going to let Bella's stupid suggestion unsettle her. Surely two adults could spend a weekend together looking after a baby without everyone thinking that there had to be something else between them.

There was no reason to suppose that Gabriel found her attractive in the slightest, Tess pointed out to herself. If Fionnula Jenkins was anything to go by, his taste was for glamorous redheads—disappointingly predictable, perhaps, but fine by *her*. She preferred her own men less dark and difficult.

Less disturbing.

Still, it was a relief when the evening was over at last. In spite of her best efforts to behave normally and keep up a flow of polite, inconsequential chat, every now and then the conversation would shrivel and die without warning, marooning them in a pool of awkward silence. Tess would find herself watching Gabriel's hands or his mouth or the pulse in his throat and the air would evaporate from her lungs and her heartbeat would boom in her ears, so loud that she'd been afraid he would hear it. And then she would gulp and plunge back into speech, not knowing or caring what she said, just desperate to break that strumming silence.

'Sorry about the mess,' she said with forced brightness when the interminable meal had ended, and she was able to show him into Andrew's room. 'It should be more comfortable than the sofa, though.'

'I'm sure it will be fine,' said Gabriel, equally constrained. 'Thank you for the meal,' he added after a moment.

'Thank *you* for all the work you did around the house this afternoon.'

Another agonizing pause.

'Well…goodnight,' she said uncomfortably, feeling that she should be saying something else, but unsure what it should be. She clasped her hands nervously in front of her.

If he had been anyone other than Gabriel, she would have hugged him with a smile and told him to sleep well.

But he *was* Gabriel, and what would have seemed so easy and so natural with a friend was somehow fraught with danger. The sensible thing was to turn and go, but something held her there, her eyes skittering around the room until drawn irresistibly back to his and she could only stand staring helplessly at him while the silence tightened around them.

She stood by the door, as if poised for flight, but the room was so small that she was still close enough for Gabriel to smell the scented bath oil that lingered on her skin, a heady fragrance of flowers and spices.

Close enough for him to kiss.

Not a real kiss, of course, Gabriel told himself. Just a friendly peck to thank her for all she had done today. Wasn't that the obvious, the appropriate, thing to do in the circumstances? He could bend his head, touch his mouth to the warm curve of her face, and that would be that. Easy.

But not as easy as reaching out and drawing her towards him, so that he could twine his fingers in her hair. Not as easy as letting his lips drift from her cheek to find her mouth. Not as easy as kissing her properly, the way he had been trying not to think about doing all evening.

Gabriel swallowed. Perhaps that brief, impersonal kiss on the cheek wouldn't be that easy after all. He made himself step deliberately back so that she was out of reach.

'Good night, Tess,' was all he said.

Things were better the next day. Tess felt as if she had somehow passed through a danger zone, and had emerged unscathed on the other side. She woke feeling calmer, the jittery feeling of the night before having vanished as if it had never been.

She had just been rattled by Bella's suggestion, she realised, remembering how she had backed carefully out of Andrew's room when Gabriel had said goodnight, unsure whether to be disappointed or relieved that he had made no move to get any closer to her. He had clearly remembered that their relationship was entirely professional, and that the intimate situation they had been forced into by Harry was only ever going to be temporary.

And that was good, of course.

Uncomfortably aware of just how close she herself had come to forgetting it, Tess could only be glad that she hadn't made a fool of herself by kissing him. But now that they both knew where they were, she told herself, everything would be fine.

And to her secret relief, she was right. It turned out to be an ordinary, lazy Sunday. Gabriel was already up and had made coffee by the time Tess went downstairs with Harry. They read the Sunday papers in companionable silence, and after lunch took him for a walk on the common nearby.

It was a raw, blustery day and the autumn leaves swirled in golden eddies along the paths. Tess turned her collar up against the wind as she walked beside Gabriel, who pushed the pram with the same decisive control that he drove the car or logged onto his computer. Studying his profile surreptitiously under her lashes, Tess couldn't help thinking how strong and definite his features were, and how everyone else they passed looked pale and insubstantial in comparison, and something that was not quite pride and not quite pleasure stirred faintly inside her.

It started to rain as they turned for home. By the time they reached Tess's street, it was pouring, and they ran the last few yards, falling breathless and laughing through the door into the warmth of the house. The hallway was so narrow that the pram almost filled it, and the two of them were wedged close together in the space between it and the front door. Gabriel shook himself, wiping the rain from his face, and turned to say something to Tess, but the words died on his lips.

Her face was glowing, her hair blown around by the wind and spangled with raindrops. The clear brown eyes were alight with laughter as she tried to catch her breath, but her smile faltered as she met his arrested gaze and for a moment the air between them shimmered with the tension they had both hoped was forgotten.

Tess turned away first. 'I'll make some tea,' she said brightly—too brightly—squeezing past the pram to the relative safety of the kitchen.

She had herself well under control by the time she carried a tray into the sitting room. Gabriel and Harry watched her as she drew the curtains to shut out the rain and the gathering darkness, and then knelt to switch on the fire. The line of her back was somehow soothing, Gabriel found himself thinking.

She had toasted crumpets to have with the tea. Gabriel hardly tasted his. He kept noticing how she licked the melted butter from her fingers, how she cupped her hands around her mug, how the firelight burnished her hair as she sat cross-legged on the rug with Harry. She had the glove puppet they had bought yesterday, and was making him chuckle by playing peekaboo with the fox, making it wave at him and then duck back into hiding behind her arm.

Gabriel's throat was absurdly dry. 'Better not get too attached to him,' he managed. 'I hope his mother will be home soon, and you'll have to give him back.'

'I know.' Tess looked at Harry, who was reaching chubby hands out for the fox. 'I wonder how she could have left him?' she said, almost to herself. 'I wouldn't if he was mine.'

Gabriel quirked an eyebrow at her. 'Getting broody?'

'No,' she said quickly, perhaps a little too quickly. 'Harry's adorable when he's like this,' she admitted, watching the baby stuff the glove puppet thoughtfully into his mouth, 'but it's not so much fun when you're changing nappies or getting up in the middle of the night. It's hard work on your own. I should know,' she said. 'I brought Andrew up by myself.'

'If you had a baby you wouldn't be on your own,' said Gabriel.

'Wouldn't I?' He had never heard her so cynical before. 'It happens all the time,' she quoted his own words back at him. 'You think you're in love and that everything's going to be wonderful—and for a while it *is* wonderful. And then you find yourself alone. You cope because you haven't got a choice.'

Tess stroked Harry's head. 'Maybe that's what Leanne had to do. Maybe that's why she left him.'

'It was her choice not to tell Greg about the baby,' Gabriel pointed out in his brother's defence.

'True.' She glanced at him. 'Will you tell him?'

'I think it's up to Harry's mother to do that.'

'Wouldn't you want to know if it was you?'

Gabriel's mouth turned down at the corners as he considered the question. 'I don't know. Probably not. I've never thought about children. The whole family business is too much of a commitment. I don't like compromise, and that's what families are all about.'

'They're about more than that,' Tess protested.

'Like what?'

'Security? Comfort? Trust? Love?'

'Oh, love...' Gabriel made a dismissive gesture. 'You can have love without being married and having children.'

'Yes, but how long does it last?' she countered sadly.

'Long enough.'

Her face closed. 'Long enough for what? For you to get bored? That's not love.'

He eyed her curiously. 'You sound as if you're speaking from experience.'

Turning her head away, Tess cradled the mug between her hands and stared into the leaping flames. 'I fell in love once,' she told him, her voice carefully expressionless. 'Oliver worked in the same office. It was my first job and he was much older, more assured. I trusted him completely, and when he told me he loved me but we had to be discreet because of his position in the company, I believed him.'

Gabriel listened, but his eyes were on the fine arch of her brows and the way her hair fell in a soft caress against her cheek and, without wanting to, he found himself wondering what it would be like to be able to reach out and smooth it gently behind her ear. It was alarming to discover just how clearly he could imagine doing just that, and he had to catch himself up sharply when he realised what he was doing.

'I was very young,' Tess was saying. 'Very young and very naïve. I never thought that the reason he was so anxious to keep our relationship quiet was the fact that he had a wife who was related to the managing director.

'It turned out that everyone knew anyway,' she went on with a bitter smile. 'You can't keep that kind of thing secret in an office. They all knew long before I did that Oliver was going to dump me and, when the director got wind of the affair and called me, they knew exactly what was going to happen.'

Her cheeks burned at the memory of that final interview. 'That was the first I'd heard about Oliver's wife. I had to leave, of course. I was expendable, and Oliver wasn't. I vowed there and then that I would never get involved with anyone at work again, and I haven't. I never mix work with my private life.'

'What about now?'

Startled by the strange note in his voice, Tess lifted her head to look at him. 'What do you mean?'

'I'm your boss, I'm here in your home. You could say I'm intruding on your private life.'

'That's different,' said Tess. 'Our relationship is professional, not personal, and that hasn't changed. I work for you during the week, and I'm working for you now. You're here because of Harry, not because you want to be here, and you're not here because I want you here. This weekend is about business, not pleasure.'

CHAPTER SEVEN

GABRIEL glared at the red light, his fingers tapping morosely on the steering wheel. It would be afternoon before they got to the office at this rate. It had taken long enough to load Harry and all his stuff into the car, and now they were stuck in the Monday morning traffic.

He blew out an irritable breath, nettled by the way Tess sat beside him, infuriatingly self-possessed. She had come downstairs that morning in one of her demure suits, with her hair swept into a neat chignon at the back of her head, looking dauntingly cool and unapproachable. Without saying a word, she had made it crystal clear that the situation was back to normal, and that relations between them were strictly business.

Gabriel knew that he ought to be relieved. The last thing he needed or wanted was to complicate matters by getting involved with his PA, and he should have been glad that she clearly had no intention of presuming on the enforced intimacy of the weekend, but somehow her composure rankled. *He* was the one who liked to keep people at arm's length.

The light turned green ahead. Muttering under his breath at the slowness of the traffic, Gabriel edged the car forward, but only managed a few yards before it changed back to red. He felt grouchy and unsettled, the way he had been feeling ever since that conversation in front of the fire. 'You're not here because I want you here,' that was what she had said. 'This weekend is about business, not pleasure.'

Gabriel's lips tightened whenever he thought about it. He had been misled by the warmth and the firelight and

113

the smile in her eyes, had forgotten that he was only there because of Harry, had forgotten the office, had forgotten that Tess was his PA. Her cool reminder that their relationship was a purely professional one had been like a slap in the face, and had left him humiliated and feeling a fool.

It wasn't a feeling Gabriel liked, and it did nothing to improve his temper. When they finally reached the office, he stiff-armed his way through the glass door and strode through reception, deaf to the receptionist's timid greeting and blind to the wary looks of those who automatically cleared a passage for him, aware only of Tess following calmly behind him with Harry.

Tess sucked in through her teeth. She had seen at once what kind of mood he was in that morning, and had intended to ignore it. She had obviously done something to upset him, but that was no reason for him to take it out on everyone else.

'Haven't you forgotten something?' she asked coldly as she caught up with him at the lifts with Harry.

'What?' Gabriel was carrying Harry's bouncy chair in one hand, and jabbing at the button to call the lift with the other.

'You made a promise on Friday night.'

Thrown off his stride, he took his finger off the button and scowled at her. 'What do you mean? What promise?'

'I'll be nice, you said. I'm desperate, you said. I'll do anything. Remember?'

Gabriel's jaw tightened. 'What am I supposed to do? Skip around dispensing sunshine and days off?'

'A simple good morning would be a step in the right direction,' said Tess in a frigid voice. 'You didn't even acknowledge Elaine's existence.'

'Since I've no idea who Elaine is, that's hardly surprising.'

'She's been the receptionist here for the last six years.

You must have seen her every day since you arrived. The least you could do is learn her name.'

Gabriel drew an exasperated breath and turned with a muttered comment that Tess chose to ignore. 'Good morning, Elaine,' he called across to where she sat behind the reception desk.

Elaine's jaw dropped. 'G-good morning, Mr S-stearne,' she stuttered.

'How are you this morning?'

'Er—fine, thank you,' she managed, looking thoroughly alarmed by his bizarre behaviour.

'Satisfied?' Gabriel demanded of Tess, who shifted Harry into her other arm and looked coolly back at him.

'It's a start.'

The lift doors slid open, revealing a number of Tess's colleagues, who all looked apprehensive at finding themselves face to face with the fearsome Gabriel Stearne, and, like Elaine, were positively unnerved when he bared his teeth in a savage smile.

'Good morning,' he said pointedly to each in turn.

There was a chorus of subdued and frankly baffled greetings in return. Tess stood next to Gabriel at the front, staring woodenly ahead, but uncomfortably aware of the knowing looks being exchanged behind her back, along with nods and winks at the significance of her arrival at the same time as Gabriel, still with the baby in tow.

There was no need to tell anyone that they had spent the weekend together, she thought with a sinking heart. Conclusions were obviously being drawn already. The news would be all round the office in no time, and the grapevine would arrive at its usual calculation that two plus two inevitably made at least sixty-seven!

It was a relief to escape the speculative eyes boring into her back and into the comparative sanctuary of her office. Gabriel stomped off into his own room, leaving Tess to settle Harry in his bouncy chair while she organised herself. He seemed happy to sit there, pulling at his socks, and watching her as she moved around her desk, but his uncle was clearly in a less amenable mood. Tess could hear him banging around in his office, slamming files onto his desk as if they were somehow responsible for his bad humour.

Gabriel, in fact, was finding it hard to concentrate and, when Tess came in with her notebook and the diary a little while later, he glared at her from behind his desk, irritated even more than usual by that air of crisp efficiency.

'Yes?' he barked.

Ignoring him, Tess consulted the diary. 'You've got a meeting at eleven-fifteen, and another at three,' she reminded him. 'John Dobbs would like to see you some time today about insurance.'

'Tell him three forty-five.'

'You're expected in the design department at four.'

'Cancel that.'

Calmly, Tess made a note.

Gabriel eyed her with a kind of baffled resentment. She was unperturbed by his black humour, just as she had been unperturbed by the weekend they had spent together. He had seen her sitting in front of the fire with her hair tumbling over her shoulders. He had seen her bathrobe slip open, seen her smiling and laughing. How could she put on a suit and some glasses and act as if he didn't know what she was really like?

She was looking at him over the top of her glasses. 'Will there be anything else for now?'

Yes, he wanted to shout. Be the way you were this weekend. Be the Tess who hummed as she stirred the soup. Be the Tess who ran through the rain. The one who made Harry laugh with that stupid fox, and took long, scented baths by candlelight.

'No, nothing,' he said curtly.

'Would you like a cup of coffee?'

'Yes.'

Tess raised an eyebrow. That was all it took. Gabriel sighed irritably.

'Yes, *please*,' he ground out. 'If you wouldn't mind.'

He had made *her* coffee yesterday morning, he remembered, glowering out of the window. They had had coffee and croissants and had chatted companionably as they'd read the Sunday papers. Not that Tess would remember that now. She was too busy being an efficient PA to waste her time actually talking to her own boss.

It annoyed Gabriel that he couldn't stop thinking about her. She was only his PA, for God's sake! There was nothing special about her, if he discounted that ability to freeze him with a look. She wasn't particularly beautiful, nor particularly stylish, nor particularly clever.

So why was he wasting his valuable time thinking of excuses to go out into the office and talk to her? Anyone would think he needed to hear her voice.

Which was ridiculous.

Knowing how ridiculous it was didn't stop him from snatching up the phone when it rang.

'Yes?'

'I've got Fionnula Jenkins on the line for you.'

Something about the utter lack of inflection in Tess's voice made Gabriel furious. She might at least sound as if she cared whether he spoke to another woman or not! The truth was that he hadn't given Fionnula a thought all weekend, but Tess wasn't to know that, was she?

'Put her through,' he ordered. 'Oh—if it's not too much trouble, of course,' he added sarcastically.

Tess refused to give him the satisfaction of rising to the bait. She connected him to Fionnula without comment, and relieved her feelings by slamming down the phone with such violence that she made Harry jump.

'I'm sorry, sweetheart,' she apologised as his little face

puckered alarmingly, and she bent to pick him up for a cuddle. 'It's not your fault your uncle is impossible.'

'Uh-oh!' said a familiar voice from the doorway. 'It looks like I picked a bad time.'

Tess turned with Harry. 'Come in, Niles,' she said, resigned.

'So this is the boss's baby.' Niles's eyes were bright with curiosity. 'He doesn't look much like Dad, does he?'

'That's because Mr Stearne isn't his father,' said Tess repressively.

'But he's looking after him, I hear—with you.'

'It's just a temporary arrangement.'

'Ah.' Niles regarded her speculatively. 'The word is that you and the boss spent the weekend together. Emma said she saw the two of you in the supermarket.'

Tess suppressed a sigh. She might have known someone would have seen them. Everyone thought that London was a big city, but there were times, usually when you most wanted to mind your own business, when it might as well be a village.

'I expect she did,' she said as coolly as she could. 'We had to get some stuff for Harry here. You can tell everyone not to get excited,' she added with an ironic look. 'There's no big secret. Harry is Mr Stearne's nephew, and I'm acting as nanny for a few days to earn some overtime. That's all there is to it.'

'Shame,' said Niles. 'I was hoping to hear you'd cut out Fionnula Jenkins!'

'I don't think that's very likely.'

'I don't know about that,' he said, studying her appreciatively. 'You're a beautiful girl, Tess, in a quiet kind of way. I reckon you could give Fionnula a run for her money if you let your hair down.'

Tess's mind flickered back to the weekend. She had a picture of herself sitting by the fire with her hair loose, and Gabriel on the sofa, leaning forward, his eyes intent,

holding Harry upright between his big hands, smiling...
The memory made her shiver for some reason, and she
pushed it hastily aside.

'Well, as you can see, my hair is firmly up,' she told
Niles briskly as she sat Harry on his mat and found a few
toys for him to play with. 'What did you want, anyway,
Niles?'

'I just stopped by to see if you'd thought any more about
the promises auction. We're relying on you to come up
with something good.'

Tess had forgotten all about the auction. 'I could do a
couple of hours ironing for you, if you like,' she offered,
improvising quickly.

'Ironing?' Niles scoffed. 'Don't be so boring, Tess. You
can do better than that.'

'Like what?' She sighed.

'Rumour has it that you're a good cook.' Niles had obviously been waiting for his opportunity. 'Why don't you
promise to cook a romantic meal for two? Lots of people
would want to bid for that.'

'Oh, all right,' said Tess, just to get rid of him, and he
grinned.

'You're a star!' He gave her an affectionate hug just as
the inner door opened and Gabriel came out.

Gabriel's mouth thinned as he saw the two of them
break apart guiltily, and Tess was furious to find herself
blushing.

'We were—er—just discussing the firm's social event
in November.'

'Really?' said Gabriel with an icy look. 'It seems to me
that quite enough socialising goes on right here in this
office.'

'I'd better get back to work,' said Niles prudently. 'See
you later, Tess—and thanks for your promise.'

The look Gabriel sent after him was distinctly hostile.
'Why is he always hanging around here?' he demanded.

Tess closed her lips firmly. She wasn't about to get into an argument. 'Is there something I can do for you?'

'Yes, you can book me a table at Cupiditas. I'm taking Fionnula out to lunch,' he told her unnecessarily. 'To make up for the meal we missed the other night.'

The other night when *she* had had to give up her evening to help look after his baby nephew, thought Tess furiously. Fionnula hadn't exactly been supportive then, had she? But all she'd had to do was ring Gabriel up with her husky voice and crook her little finger, and he came running. He ought to have more pride, thought Tess austerely.

'What time?' was all she said.

'Twelve-thirty. Fionnula's going to meet me here. I'm sure you'll look after her if I'm late back from the meeting,' he added with what Tess strongly suspected was deliberate provocation.

'Of course, Mr Stearne,' she said, her voice empty of expression.

'*Gabriel*,' he bit out.

'Of course, Gabriel,' she corrected herself after the tiniest of pauses.

Gabriel cast her a fulminating look and slammed back into his room, infuriated to discover that she had succeeded in provoking him far more effectively than he had in irritating her. He had only asked Fionnula to lunch to prove to Tess that he too could behave as if they had never spent the weekend together. Not that she cared one way or another: she couldn't even remember to use his first name.

He was still looking thunderous when he left for his meeting, and Tess told herself that she was glad to see him go. At least now she might be able to get some work done without him prowling around the office. Even Harry had picked up on his black temper, and what with trying to soothe one and placate the other, she had achieved virtually nothing.

But somehow it wasn't any easier when he had gone.

The office felt empty without him, and Tess was annoyed to find herself looking up quickly every time the lift doors pinged out in the corridor in case it was Gabriel returning.

Rather to Tess's surprise, Fionnula turned up bang on time. She paused dramatically in the doorway and shook back her famous red hair. 'Is Gabriel here?' she asked in the equally famous throaty voice. She didn't introduce herself, evidently assuming that Tess would recognise her straight away.

Tess longed to pretend that she didn't, but had to force a polite smile instead. 'I'm sorry, he's still in a meeting, but he is expecting you,' she said. 'He asked me to apologise if he was a little late. Can I get you a coffee or anything in the meantime?'

'No thank you, darling, I'll wait until lunch.' Fionnula shrugged off her expensive-looking jacket and dropped it carelessly over a chair. 'I hope Gabriel's booked somewhere nice?'

'Cupiditas,' Tess admitted grudgingly. She had had to spend some time persuading the manager to find a table for two at such short notice.

'Oh, marvellous!' Fionnula looked smug. 'He knows that's my favourite.'

In the flesh, Fionnula was even more beautiful than in photographs, Tess had to acknowledge. There was a glow about her, a sheen of sheer glamour that went beyond the flawless skin, green, green eyes, and stunning figure. Her hair was a deep, coppery red, without so much as a hint of carrot, and Tess knew that she must look prim and colourless in comparison. No wonder Gabriel had fallen over himself to take her out again.

Unaccountably depressed, Tess forced her attention back to her computer, but the next moment Fionnula had spied Harry, kicking and gurgling quietly in his bouncy chair. 'Oh, what an adorable baby!' she cried, swooping down on him and scooping him up into her arms. 'Gabriel didn't tell me what a gorgeous boy you were,' she told him, tickling his face with her long eyelashes until he squirmed and giggled.

Tess watched, obscurely hurt to see Harry so easily won over by Fionnula's beauty and charm. Men! She sighed to herself. They were all the same!

She stared fixedly at the computer screen, bitterly aware of Fionnula, who was now dandling him on her knee, tickling and flirting until Harry was enslaved like all the others.

The two of them made a perfect picture when Gabriel walked into the office some fifteen minutes later. Fionnula was holding Harry above her, while he gazed adoringly down into her face. Tess had been silently willing him to be sick over Fionnula's cashmere top, but to her disappointment he was behaving beautifully and, at the sight of Gabriel, both of them lit up on cue.

Which was more than Tess did, Gabriel noted sourly. She had barely looked up from her computer screen.

'There you are, darling!' Still holding Harry, the perfect, radiant, mother figure, Fionnula moved towards him with a brilliant smile.

Behind her, Gabriel was almost sure that he had seen Tess's lips tighten fractionally. A reaction at last! It was enough to make him greet Fionnula with extra warmth.

'I'm sorry to have kept you waiting,' he said, kissing her deliberately. 'I hope Tess has been looking after you.'

'She's been *marvellous*,' husked Fionnula, who had pretty much ignored Tess's existence since she had latched onto Harry. 'What a treasure you are,' she added graciously to Tess, who stared woodenly at her screen.

'I see you've met Harry,' said Gabriel, drawing Fionnula's attention back from Tess.

'Oh, I'm utterly, utterly in love with him,' Fionnula declared in her husky voice, and laughed delightedly as

Harry snuggled into her shoulder. 'You're my ideal man, aren't you, precious?'

She laid her free hand on Gabriel's arm and smiled bewitchingly up under those lashes. 'Well, one of them, anyway,' she murmured.

For a fleeting moment, Gabriel met Tess's eyes over the top of her glasses, before both looked away.

'We'd better go,' he said abruptly to Fionnula, who hung back, still playing the role of devoted mother.

'I'm not sure I can bear to leave Harry,' she said, pouting. 'Can we take him with us?'

Gabriel frowned. 'I don't think Cupiditas take children.'

As Fionnula must know full well, thought Tess dourly. If she was that thrilled with Harry, let her feed him between bites of a sandwich, which was obviously what *she* was going to have to do.

A pair of huge green eyes turned on her. 'Then, perhaps Tess...?' She held Harry out with a show of reluctance.

Tess took off her glasses and rose to her feet. 'I'll look after him,' she said, taking the baby back.

'Oh, *thank* you,' Fionnula gushed, as if Harry were her responsibility.

'There's no need to thank me,' said Tess, very cool. 'Mr Stearne is paying me to look after Harry.'

Mr Stearne is paying me. Gabriel mimicked her accent savagely to himself as he waited for the lift with Fionnula. As if he ever got a chance to forget it!

Disgruntled and restless, he was already regretting having invited Fionnula out to lunch. What was wrong with him? Gabriel wondered, the third time he found himself sneaking a surreptitious glance at his watch. Fionnula was beautiful, talented, sexy. Most men would give anything to be in his position, with her hand covering his, and the green eyes gazing seductively into his face. They wouldn't be wasting their time mentally comparing her with their PA, would they?

But Gabriel couldn't help it. Fionnula smouldered, Tess was cool and restrained. Fionnula was flamboyant, Tess precise. Fionnula was stunningly beautiful, and Tess... Tess was just Tess.

And Fionnula wanted him. Tess didn't.

So, when a box of chocolates caught his eye on his way back to the office, why did he waste his time going into the shop and buying them for Tess?

'These are for you,' he said gruffly, practically shoving the box across the desk towards her.

Tess, who had spent the lunch hour trying not to think about Gabriel and Fionnula and feeling out of sorts, stared at the chocolates.

Unthinkingly, she got to her feet, clutching the box to her chest. 'For me?' she asked incredulously.

'You said they were your favourites.' He sounded almost defensive.

'They are...but...why are you giving me chocolates?' asked Tess, completely thrown by the unexpected gesture.

Yes, *why*? Gabriel asked himself savagely. 'They're a thank you for looking after Harry,' he said after an infinitesimal pause.

'You're paying me for doing that,' she pointed out, embarrassed.

'Yes, I know I'm paying you,' he said grouchily. 'This is extra, all right? You don't have to have them! I just saw them and I thought of you—'

He stopped, uncomfortably aware of revealing more than he wanted. There was no reason why a box of chocolates should conjure up such a vivid picture of Tess sitting on the floor of his apartment, her beautiful hair tucked behind her ears and her eyes closed in blissful anticipation as she popped a chocolate in her mouth.

Suddenly self-conscious, he hunched an irritable shoulder. 'It's come to something when you have to justify thanking your secretary,' he grumbled. 'You were the one who told me I ought to show more appreciation.'

It was true. She had said that. She just hadn't known how disconcerting it would be when he took her advice. Tess could feel a treacherous glow spreading inside. Rarely had a gift been presented with less charm, but that didn't matter. He had thought about her. He had remembered which chocolates were her favourite.

And he hadn't spent long over lunch with Fionnula. That meant most of all.

'Thank you,' she said simply.

Gabriel hesitated. 'I know I can be difficult sometimes,' he acknowledged grudgingly.

Sometimes? thought Tess.

'I'm getting used to it,' she said.

And the worst thing was that it was true.

Gabriel's expression relaxed for the first time that day. He smiled at her and, without quite meaning to, Tess found herself smiling back until both became aware of the charge in the air and stopped abruptly at exactly the same time.

There was a pause which felt awkward for some reason. Tess's gaze dropped to her desk and she busied herself tidying some papers that were already neatly laid out.

She cleared her throat. 'Is it all right with you if I leave early this afternoon?' she asked after a moment. 'I'd like to get Harry home before the rush hour.'

'I'll drive you,' Gabriel offered.

'No,' she said quickly. 'I mean...there's no need. We can get a taxi. Harry slept pretty well last night,' she went on carefully, still straightening papers. 'I can manage him by myself now.' She forced a smile but didn't meet his eyes. 'I might as well earn that overtime. There's no point in you being there as well. I'm sure there are other things you'd rather be doing than changing nappies.'

There were, of course, Gabriel insisted to himself as he prowled restlessly around his apartment that night. Tess was right. He hadn't been much use with Harry, and why should he spend his time changing nappies and making up bottles when he was paying her to do it? He had better things to do.

Here he was, at the peak of his profession, he reminded himself. He had taken over an ailing company, and there was every reason to believe that he could turn it into a thriving concern, as a step towards moving into the rest of Europe. He had lots of money, a smart car, a convenient apartment. *Two* convenient apartments, he amended, remembering his home in New York. He was free, in his prime. He went out with beautiful women. What more, Gabriel asked himself, could he possibly want?

Surely it had to be something more exciting than a small warm house and Tess, barefoot and smiling, with her hair tumbling softly around her face?

Gabriel looked around the apartment that seemed suddenly cold and characterless, and he frowned. He had to stop thinking about Tess. Complications of that kind were the last thing he wanted. Building up the business was his priority, and he needed Tess as his PA. He didn't believe in office relationships any more than she did.

Not that there was any question of…whatever. Tess wasn't his type, and he clearly wasn't hers. She had made it plain that she was quite happy on her own.

Just like he was.

And he *was*, Gabriel told himself. Perfectly happy.

On the other side of the river, Tess was reassuring herself that she had done the right thing. Gabriel's lunch date with Fionnula had left her feeling unaccountably disgruntled, and she had been determined to show him that she could manage Harry without any help from him. If he wanted to spend his time going out with Fionnula, that was up to him. She didn't need him. She would be fine on her own. Absolutely fine.

But then Gabriel had come back with the chocolates,

and he had smiled, and her dudgeon had faded, only to be replaced by something much more dangerous, something alarmingly close to liking, and that would never do. With her house to herself again, it would be much easier to remember all the reasons why she didn't really like him at all, and why she didn't care *who* he had lunch with.

Only it wasn't really easier at all. Gabriel's absence was nearly as disturbing as his presence. Tess kept turning round, expecting to see him. Every time she went through a door, she would look at the handle and think about how competently he had fixed it into place with his strong, square hands, the same hands that had curved over her body, and a strange feeling would slither down her spine.

Tess told herself that she was being silly. It was inevitable that she and Gabriel had got to know each other better over the course of the weekend, but nothing had changed. Sitting disconsolately in front of the fire that night, she remembered what she had said about keeping her private and professional lives quite distinct. The longer Gabriel had stayed, the harder that would have been to do. Yes, it was much better this way.

It didn't stop the house feeling very empty that night, though.

Using the meagre information he had from Greg, Gabriel had briefed a firm of private investigators to find Harry's mother as quickly as possible but, as the days passed without any word, they began to fall into a new routine in the office.

Every morning, Tess brought Harry in after his breakfast. For the most part, he was happy to sit in his chair, or play with his toys on the mat, and let himself be fussed over by everyone who came into the office. Tess was just grateful he wasn't yet at the crawling stage and it was easy enough to keep an eye on him.

When he got bored, she took him on her lap and let him

smack his hands onto her keyboard, or inspect the strange objects on her desk. Everything went into Harry's mouth. She was constantly rescuing things from his grasp, and soon learned to remove pens and paperclips out of reach of those curious little hands.

Using the phone wasn't a problem, once she had explained the source of the chatty babbling in the background, but she only really managed to get any work done when Harry was sleeping. The other secretaries helped her out a lot, and sometimes, if she needed to do something urgently, Gabriel would take him and walk him round the office, although actually Tess found it even harder to concentrate when he was there. Harry awake was less of a distraction.

Tess didn't like the fact that she was so aware of Gabriel. It wasn't like her to be unsettled like this. She had done her very best to put the memory of waking up in bed with him to the back of her mind, but it wouldn't go away no matter how hard she tried to convince herself that it had been no more than an embarrassing incident that was better forgotten.

She would think that she *had* forgotten it, only to find that the memories were waiting to ambush her at the least appropriate moment. Gabriel would be dictating or demanding a file or shouting down the phone, and Tess would catch her breath at the thought of his lips and his hands and his hard body.

Gabriel himself seemed to be making an effort to be as difficult and demanding as normal, and he only let down his guard with the baby, and only when he thought no one was looking. Outwardly, he was brusque with Harry, but once or twice Tess caught him playing with him in his inner office, tossing him in the air until he squealed, or tickling his tummy. The moment he realised that she was watching him, he would stop, covering his embarrassment with bluster, and Tess would pretend that she hadn't noticed.

By Thursday, Harry was part of the office. Tess couldn't remember what it was like to settle down to work without having to stop to feed him or change him or let him stand on her knees and explore her face with glee.

When the phone rang that afternoon, Tess had him on her hip as she stood at the filing cabinets, searching one-handed for a document Gabriel wanted. Carrying Harry back over to the desk, she picked up the receiver.

It was Elaine. 'There's a Leanne Morrison in reception,' she told Tess doubtfully. 'She says she has to see Mr Stearne. It's urgent, she says.'

Tess had a weird sense of *déjà vu*. She had been here before, she thought with an odd, detached part of her mind.

'Send her up,' she said slowly.

She knocked on Gabriel's door. 'What is it?' he said, as if having to remind himself to be irritable.

'Harry's mother is on her way up.'

Gabriel stared at her. 'Why didn't the investigators tell us that they had found her?'

'I don't think they did,' said Tess. 'I think Leanne has found us.'

CHAPTER EIGHT

LEANNE wasn't at all Tess's idea of a croupier. She had softly curling blonde hair and a sweet expression overlaid with anxiety. Hesitating in the doorway, her big blue eyes swept around the office until they saw the baby in Tess's arms.

'Harry!' she said in a choked voice, and Tess's throat tightened as his little face lit up at the sight of his mother. Leanne clutched him to her, murmuring his name over and over again, oblivious to anyone else.

It was some time before Leanne could speak. 'I'm so sorry,' she said at last, her eyes still brimming with tears. 'I got a flight home as soon as Mum told me what she'd done. I've come straight from Heathrow. I was terrified he wouldn't be here,' she went on, hugging Harry close. 'I can't tell you what a relief it is to see him.'

'He's been quite safe,' Tess reassured her.

'I can see that.' Leanne managed a wavering smile. 'I shouldn't have left him, I know, but I needed the money, and it was only for six weeks...I can't believe what Mum did. She had no right to go to Gabriel.'

She squared her shoulders. 'I'd better see Gabriel and explain,' she said. 'Is he here?'

Gabriel, who had been watching Harry's reunion with his mother with a distant expression that effectively concealed how moved he felt, glanced at Tess. 'I'm Gabriel,' he said.

Leanne looked confused. 'I'm sorry, I meant Gabriel Stearne.'

'That's my name.' Picking his words with care, Gabriel explained how the misunderstanding had arisen. It was hard to excuse his brother's deception, but Leanne had obviously got to know Greg quite well in a short time, because she didn't seem that surprised. 'Greg still doesn't know about Harry,' he finished. 'I think you should be the one to tell him.'

'I should have told him before,' Leanne said with a sigh. 'But I didn't think he'd want to know. He was so charming and such fun,' she remembered a little wistfully, 'but he never pretended that he was serious. It was my choice to have Harry, not his and I didn't think it was fair to expect him to take any responsibility for him.'

Remorsefully, she looked from Gabriel to Tess. 'It turns out that you've taken responsibility for Harry instead. I'm sorry.'

'We've enjoyed it,' said Tess, realising for the first time that it was true. 'We're going to miss Harry.' She sent Gabriel a look, willing him to help her reassure Leanne. 'Aren't wc?' she added pointedly.

He met her look. 'Yes,' he said after a fractional pause. 'We are. You're tired,' he went on, uncomfortable with all the emotional undercurrents. Leanne looked close to tears, and Tess didn't look much more in control. 'I'll drive you to Tess's house,' he said roughly. 'You can pick up Harry's things and I'll take you both home.'

In the end, Tess persuaded Leanne to spend the night, since her mother was still away and she was too jet-lagged and emotional to cope on her own. 'You can sleep in the spare room,' she said. 'Take Harry home tomorrow.'

'I'll send a car for you,' said Gabriel, getting to his feet, glad that it was all sorted out. 'I'd better go,' he added to Tess.

Leanne looked surprised. 'Aren't you staying? I thought you two were…' She made a gesture linking them.

'No,' they both said quickly.

Tess's cheeks were burning as she showed Gabriel out,

and she avoided his eyes. 'See you tomorrow,' she said stiltedly.

Leanne was full of apologies when she went back into the sitting room. 'I just assumed you two were together,' she tried to explain. 'It was the way you looked at each other.'

'There's nothing like that.' Tess forced a bright smile. 'Gabriel is just my boss.'

And that was *all* he was, she had to keep reminding herself over the next few days.

Gabriel was very brisk the next morning. 'I've arranged for your overtime to be added to your salary this month,' he told her, omitting to mention that he had doubled the amount they had agreed. 'I'm going to see my stepfather this weekend, but I'll be back next Wednesday. Perhaps then we can get back to normal.'

Tess couldn't quite remember what normal *was* any more. The office felt very dreary when she went in on Monday. I'm just missing Harry, she told herself. It's got nothing to do with the fact that Gabriel isn't here.

All day long, people trooped into her office and congratulated her on his absence. 'It's so much more relaxed when he's not around, isn't it?' they said, and Tess agreed, although she didn't think that it was true. She certainly didn't feel relaxed. She was edgy and irritable, and she couldn't settle to anything. Gabriel had told her that he would ring from New York and she found herself waiting for his call, jumping whenever the phone went.

As it turned out, he sent her an e-mail instead, telling her that he wouldn't be back until the following Monday after all. 'You know why, don't you?' smirked Niles when he heard the news.

'He said he had a few things to sort out in New York.'

'Right, and one of those things has long red hair and green eyes.'

Tess frowned. 'What do you mean?'

'Don't you ever read the gossip columns, Tess? Fionnula Jenkins is in New York too at the moment. Our Gabriel probably wants to keep an eye on the competition. If you're talking to him, remind him he said he'd come to the promises auction, will you?' Niles went on, oblivious to the sick, hollow feeling inside Tess. 'We're relying on him.'

Tess couldn't care less about the promises auction right then. The news that Fionnula was in New York had made her furious, and not knowing why she felt so angry only made it worse. When Gabriel eventually deigned to come back, she was very cool to him. Not that he noticed nor cared. If anything he was in a worse mood than before he'd left.

Perhaps Fionnula was giving him the run-around, thought Tess unsympathetically. He was certainly working hard to impress her. Tess seemed to spend her whole time sending flowers to Fionnula, booking tables for two, or arranging limousines to ferry them to and from glittering parties. She couldn't imagine how Gabriel got on there. He was too dark and glowering to fit into that sparkling, superficial world, and it was impossible to picture him cruising a room, gossiping and air-kissing and showing off.

He had been much more comfortable tramping across the common in the rain, she was sure. Sometimes Tess thought about the weekend they had spent together and wondered if she had imagined it all. Gabriel gave no sign that he remembered pottering around her house, or playing with Harry, or buying her chocolates. It was as if that brief moment of warmth had never happened. He was curt with her to the point of rudeness, and his face shuttered whenever he looked at her.

Tess told herself she didn't care.

For the first time, she was conscious of a sense of dissatisfaction with her life. She was tired of being efficient, tired of trailing home to an empty house every night. She had kept in touch with Leanne, and was surprised at how much she enjoyed seeing Harry again, but she wanted something more. She wanted to go out and enjoy herself.

She wanted to forget about Gabriel and the way things had been when Harry had been there.

So when her old boss, Steve Robinson, rang one evening and asked her out to dinner, Tess jumped at the chance. 'Put on your glad rags,' said Steve. 'We're dining in style!'

'We are? What's the occasion?'

'I've got a proposition to put to you.'

He wouldn't tell her any more then, but Tess took him at his word, and rifled through her wardrobe in search of something suitably glamorous to wear, settling eventually on a dress that she had bought in the summer sales. It was a softer style than she usually wore, but she loved the deep gold fabric that brought out the colour of her eyes and flattered her figure. She brushed out her hair so that it fell gleaming to her shoulders and slipped her feet into high heels that were impossible to walk more than a few yards in but which made her feel wonderful. She was ready to hit the town.

Steve whistled when he saw her and his obvious appreciation was balm to Tess's sore spirit after a week of being ignored or snapped at by Gabriel. To her relief, Steve had come in a taxi, so they could go door to door.

'On behalf of my feet, I thank you,' said Tess, looking ruefully down at her unsuitable shoes as she settled into the back of the taxi. 'This is all very grand, Steve. Where are we going?'

'Cupiditas,' he told her with a grin.

'Cupiditas?' she echoed in a hollow voice. 'What a great idea!'

It was a horrible idea. Tess had taken a dislike to the very idea of Cupiditas ever since discovering that it was Fionnula's favourite restaurant, and the last thing she wanted tonight was to be reminded of Gabriel, as she inevitably would be. She had booked him so many tables there, she knew the telephone number off by heart.

At least she knew Gabriel and Fionnula wouldn't be there, Tess reassured herself. Gabriel had asked—ordered—her to book another restaurant for tonight.

'I thought you'd be pleased,' said Steve. 'I wanted to give you a real treat.'

Cupiditas had such a starry reputation that Tess half expected them to be turned away at the door for not being beautiful or famous enough, but they were shown to a table on the far side of the crowded room. The whole place reeked of money and glamour, and Tess was sinkingly aware of how much the evening would cost Steve.

'This is wonderful,' she said dutifully as they sat down.

A waiter was hovering to present the menus with a flourish. Tess smiled her thanks up at him as she accepted hers, and she was still smiling when he moved away and she found herself looking over Steve's shoulder at the table which had been blocked from her view, and where a man sat staring back at her.

Gabriel.

Shock wiped the smile from Tess's face, and stopped her heart in mid beat. She was paralysed, skewered by the expression in his eyes which managed to blaze and freeze at the same time, and all she could do was stare helplessly back at him, as if the two of them were quite alone, and the other diners had retreated into the far distance, cut off by an invisible wall of silence.

Steve's hand waving in front of her face jerked Tess back to reality. 'Are you all right?' he said, watching her quizzically.

Tess pulled herself together with an effort and swallowed. 'Yes, yes, I'm fine,' she said, but her hands were unsteady as she bent her head over the menu.

The words swam in front of her eyes. Her heart was

thumping painfully in her chest and she drew a shaky breath, struggling to get a grip of herself. Steve had obviously gone to a lot of trouble and expense to make this a special evening for her. She couldn't get up and run out the way she would like to do.

Forcing a bright smile, she kept her gaze fixed on Steve's face as he talked about the company where he now worked, but all the time she was conscious of Fionnula's coppery hair cascading down her back, of her silvery laugh and extravagant gestures. And of Gabriel sitting opposite her, a dark, intense presence in the middle of the room. It took every ounce of Tess's will not to look directly at him, but his still figure tugged insistently, inexorably at the corner of her eye.

Preoccupied with the effort of not succumbing to its lure, it took Tess a little time to realise that Steve was offering her a job.

'I told you I had a proposition for you,' he said.

'But—haven't you got a PA?' Tess stammered, wishing that she had paid more attention to what he was saying.

Steve looked at her strangely. Obviously he had spent some time explaining all this. 'It's not a PA job,' he repeated patiently. 'It's not that I wouldn't like to work with you again, of course, but you're capable of so much more, Tess. It's time you spread your wings. We need an office manager to oversee the move into a new headquarters, and I think you'd be fantastic.'

'I don't know what to say.' Tess stalled, fiddling with her fork.

'I thought of you as soon as the job came up. I knew you weren't very happy working with Gabriel Stearne and were looking for a chance to move on. This is it!'

Tess bit her lip. She had told everyone she didn't like Gabriel and that she wanted to leave as soon as she found a job that paid as well. She had said it so often, she had thought it was true.

But it wasn't.

Involuntarily, she looked over Steve's shoulder, and her eyes encountered Gabriel's across the room for a charged moment before they fell back to her plate.

He was impossible, demanding, unpredictable, but she didn't dislike him. And she didn't want to leave him.

The truth settled like a stone in Tess's stomach. Why did she have to realise it now? she wondered with something close to resentment. Why couldn't she carry on hating him the way she had before? Everything had been so much easier then.

'Well, what do you say?' Steve was asking eagerly.

'I...I'll have to think about it, Steve.'

She could tell that he was disappointed by her lack of enthusiasm, and exerted herself to make up for it by chatting with feverish gaiety for the rest of the evening and pretending to enjoy the treat he had arranged for her. She exclaimed over every exquisite plate that was set before her and marvelled at how delicious the food was, although it might as well have been made of cardboard.

Gabriel wasn't enjoying his food either. He was shaken off balance by the way Tess looked. He had hardly recognised her when she'd walked in, wearing a dress in some soft, deep gold material that clung to her figure. He had seen her in a suit, seen her in jeans, he had even seen her in her satin nightdress, but he had never seen her dressed up before, and now he couldn't keep his eyes off her.

She looked fabulous, he thought, his throat tightening at the sight of her, warm and glowing with that soft, silky tumble of hair. Gabriel watched her with something close to resentment. He had spent his entire time back in the States trying to forget her, staying longer than he intended in the hope of putting her out of his mind, and when he had run into Fionnula in New York, it had seemed like the perfect opportunity to convince himself that he had.

Tess had been back to her old frigid self when he'd

eventually returned, which had made it easy for Gabriel to
let himself believe that the whole business with Harry had
never happened, and that he had never glimpsed the warm,
vibrant woman who lived behind his PA's cool mask.

And now Tess had spoilt everything by walking into
Cupiditas looking like that.

He could see all the other men in the restaurant checking
her out, but Tess only had eyes for Steve Robinson.
Gabriel remembered *him* all right. Tess's boss, the one she
had liked working for so much, before he had come along
and broken up their cosy company. *Steve was fantastic.*
Wasn't that what she had said? *He's a very nice man.*

Was she in love with him? Gabriel wondered savagely.
She certainly thought he was something special, judging
by the way she had leant towards him, her chin propped
in one hand, smiling that smile of hers, *laughing* with him.

Gabriel wanted to go over and punch him.

Signalling abruptly for the bill, he waited for Fionnula
to return from another remorseless round of table-hopping.
'Let's go,' he said.

He was determined not to mention the fact that he had
seen her the next day. What Tess did out of the office was
entirely her own business. He didn't care where she went
or who she was with as long as she did her job properly.
So when he called her into his office that morning, he was
resolutely businesslike, firing off a ream of memos and
letters, while inwardly congratulating himself on his indifference.

Tess's pen raced over the page to keep up as Gabriel
paced around the room, apparently filled with a restless
energy. It was a relief when he paused at last by the window and stood looking out, shoulders hunched and hands
thrust deep into his trouser pockets. She flexed her fingers
surreptitiously.

'I didn't realise you were still seeing Steve Robinson.'

The words were out before Gabriel could stop them, and Tess stiffened at the hostility in his tone.

'I don't have to account to you for what I do or who I see in my time off,' she said coldly.

Gabriel swung round. 'Does he often take you to places like Cupiditas?'

'Why? Is there some rule that secretaries aren't allowed?'

'Of course not,' he said irritably. 'I was just surprised to see you there.'

'I was surprised to see *you*. I'd booked you a table at the Dorchester.'

'Fionnula changed her mind.' Gabriel was annoyed to find himself explaining. 'She knows the owner of Cupiditas, so he found us a table.'

Tess's lips tightened. If it was that easy for Fionnula to get in, why did she have to spend so much of her time on the phone booking tables at Cupiditas? 'How convenient for you,' she said between her teeth.

Gabriel took another turn around the room. 'Is he married?' he asked abruptly.

'Who? Steve?'

He sucked in his breath. 'Yes, *Steve*,' he said, controlling his temper with an effort.

'Why do you ask?' Tess was obviously determined not to be helpful.

'He looks married.'

'As a matter of fact, he's divorced,' she told him frostily. 'Not that it's any of your business.'

Gabriel knew that it wasn't, but he was in the grip of some strange compulsion. 'I thought you didn't believe in mixing work and your private life?' he said accusingly.

'I don't.' The eyes that had once reminded him of warm honey were cold and clear. 'But, then, I don't work with Steve any more,' she added deliberately, and Gabriel glowered.

'No, you work for *me*, and please don't forget it. I don't want you passing any confidential information onto Steve Robinson while you're playing footsie under the table. He works for a rival organisation, so don't forget that either!'

Tess stared at him coldly. 'Steve and I have got better things to talk about than work, I can assure you,' she said.

Which wasn't really what Gabriel wanted to hear.

'Going out again?' Gabriel's voice was hard as he watched Tess hang up the dress she had brought into the office that morning.

'It's the promises auction tonight,' she said, taking off her coat. 'We're all supposed to be at the hotel at seven, so it's not worth me going home. I've brought everything I need to change here.'

She eyed him under her lashes, wondering what sort of mood he was in today. She didn't understand Gabriel at the moment. He hadn't mentioned Steve again, but he had been restless and on edge. One minute he would bite her head off, the next she would look up to find him watching her with an expression that made the breath dry in her throat.

Tess sighed inwardly. There wasn't much point in trying to understand Gabriel when she didn't even understand herself. Steve had offered her the perfect opportunity to step up the career ladder, but she kept putting off the moment of decision. They were busy in the office again and, whatever else working with Gabriel might be like, it was never boring. There was an edge to the atmosphere when he was around, a crackle to the air, that compensated for his unpredictable temper.

'Oh, *that*.' Gabriel grunted as he found the report he was looking for on her desk. 'I don't have to go, do I?'

'I think it would be a nice gesture,' said Tess coolly. 'You did promise.'

'What?' His head lifted abruptly. 'I promised? When?'

'You told Niles you would come.'

'I said I'd do my best. That's not a promise.'

'And you promised me.' Tess hadn't really wanted to remind Gabriel of their weekend together, but she knew that Niles was relying on him to turn up. 'You sat on my sofa and promised you would go to the office party if I helped you with Harry—and I did.'

'Oh, very well,' he grumbled, 'but I wish you'd reminded me about this before.'

'It's in the diary,' she pointed out crisply, 'and I sent you an e-mail the day before yesterday.'

Gabriel eyed her with dislike. When she was like this, it was hard to understand why he spent so much time trying not to think about her.

'What do I have to do at this auction?'

'I've no idea,' said Tess, switching on her computer and flicking through the post that had been left on her desk. 'Niles has promised something on your behalf, but I expect it will just be a question of writing a cheque. All you need to do is turn up, and make a generous bid for somebody's promise. And look as if you're pleased to be there. It's a party. This is a chance for staff to get to know you. You're a distant figure at the moment, and most people are scared stiff of you.'

The boss from hell, in fact. Gabriel dropped the report back on her desk where it landed with a resounding slap. 'Well, if I'm going, you'd better buy me a fresh shirt at lunch-time,' he said, getting his own back. 'I'm tied up with meetings all day, and I'm having lunch at the bank. You know my size.'

Gabriel was late back from his afternoon meeting and barely had he walked through the door when an urgent call from the New York office sent them into a whirl of activity. It was half past six by the time the crisis had been sorted out, and the rest of the staff had already set out for the hotel where the auction was due to start at seven.

Very aware that the two of them were to all intents and purposes alone in the empty building, Tess took her dress down from its hook and picked up her bag. 'I'd better go and change,' she said with forced brightness.

Gabriel didn't even look up from the letters he was signing. 'Use my bathroom if you like,' he said.

It was certainly more luxurious than the ladies', thought Tess as she zipped herself into the gold dress once more. She looked at the marble counter where they had changed Harry together. She remembered how startled she had been by Gabriel's smile, how taken aback to find herself noticing his hands. How long ago it seemed now!

For some reason, the memory unsettled her, and she was conscious of a fluttery, stupidly nervous feeling as she made up her face and slipped on her unsuitable shoes. They were getting quite a lot of wear nowadays, she reflected. Brushing out her hair vigorously, she tossed it back and eyed her reflection dubiously. She looked wide-eyed and excited, as if she were getting ready to go out on a date instead of making a dutiful appearance at a work function.

On an impulse, she swept her hair back and pinned it up with clips in her usual style. That was better. She looked more like herself. She looked poised and in control. She felt in control. She *was* in control.

Emerging from the bathroom, she surprised Gabriel in the middle of shrugging himself into the clean shirt she had bought him earlier that day, the packaging scattered over his desk. Tempted as she had been to present him with something pink and frilly to wear, in the end she had chosen a classic deep blue shirt that would go with his tie.

He looked up as she appeared, and his hands stilled at his shirt. There was a taut silence.

'Sorry,' muttered Tess, averting her eyes from his chest.

Gabriel cleared his throat. 'I'll just have a wash. We might as well go together.' He nodded in the direction of the bar in the corner of his office. 'Have a drink while you're waiting.'

Tess helped herself to a glass of wine, not because she wanted it, but for something to do with her hands. She felt jittery, on edge. Her heart was pumping, and a mixture of tension and an unaccountable excitement shivered just beneath her skin. The office was very quiet, and when she looked down on the crowds still thronging the streets far below, they seemed to belong to a different world altogether.

The sound of the bathroom door opening made her heart lurch, and she spilled her wine, only just missing her dress.

'This shirt you bought,' Gabriel was saying, holding out his arms so that she could see the cuffs flapping, 'needs cuff-links.'

'Oh, dear, ' said Tess guiltily. She hadn't even thought to look at the cuffs. 'Haven't you got any?'

'Not with me. I'll have to get some on the way.'

She looked at her watch. 'We haven't got time. We're going to be late as it is.'

'Well, I can't go like this!'

Tess put down her glass. 'We'll just have to improvise.' Glad of something to do, she went out to her own desk and rummaged in her draw until she found some treasury tags she used for filing. 'These might work.'

Gabriel eyed them in disbelief. 'What the...?'

'Look,' she said, demonstrating how the two short metal bars were linked by a green cord. 'They'd be better than nothing, anyway.'

'Well, I'll have a go,' he said, resigned, and held out his hand.

Tess selected two of the tags and passed them to him

but, as their fingers brushed, she felt a jolt that made her jerk her hand back, and the tags dropped to the floor.

Scarlet, she knelt to retrieve them. 'Sorry,' she mumbled, and took care this time to drop them into Gabriel's open palm without touching him at all.

Muttering under his breath, Gabriel managed to fasten the left cuff with one of the tags, but he fumbled with the right until he admitted defeat and asked Tess to help him. 'Otherwise we'll never get to this auction,' he said.

He held out his wrist, and Tess had no option but to stand very close to him. She bent her head over the cuff and tried to concentrate, but her fingers were unwieldy and she was distracted by his nearness, by the crazy inclination to put her arms around his waist and lean into his hard, strong body, to rest her face against his throat and smell his skin.

'It—it's not as easy as it looks, is it?' she stammered.

'No,' Gabriel answered absently. He was looking down at the clips that held the silky hair in place and imagining how it would feel to pull them loose. Her perfume was making his head spin.

This was *Tess*, he kept telling himself. His PA. She was out of bounds. She didn't believe in office relationships, and neither did he.

But he still wanted to kiss her.

Wrenching his eyes from her hair, Gabriel stared resolutely over the top of her head, but now the deep leather sofa was directly in his line of vision, and all he could think about was how easy it would be to sink down on it with her, to persuade her not to go to this stupid auction but stay there with him, just the two of them in the dark office...

'There, I think that's it.'

Tess's words made him look down, just at the moment that she looked up into his face, her fingers still on his cuff, and their eyes met. It was a mistake. The air leaked from his lungs and his throat tightened, while the silence thrummed between them, vibrant with temptation.

Tess's heart was slamming against her ribs. She wanted to move, to let her hands fall from his wrist, to say something bright and normal to banish the terrible tension, but she couldn't. She couldn't do anything but stand like a fool and stare up into his eyes.

He's going to kiss me, she thought, and was afraid. Afraid that he would, afraid that he wouldn't, afraid more than anything of her own response if he did.

Very slowly, Gabriel lifted his hands, and Tess caught her breath with a mixture of exhilaration and something like terror as she waited for him to cup her face and touch his lips to hers. He really was going to kiss her.

But he didn't. His hands hesitated for the merest fraction of a second on either side of her jaw before continuing upwards to find the clips in her hair.

'You looked better in this dress when your hair was down,' he said, a ragged edge to his voice, and he pulled the clips free to let her hair slither and bounce to her shoulders.

The temptation to cast the clips aside and wind the shining strands around his fingers, to hold her head still while he bent to kiss her, was so strong that it took all of Gabriel's will-power to step back.

'Just my opinion, of course.'

He held out the clips. Moistening her lips, Tess took them with unsteady fingers. 'We'd better go,' she said huskily.

She put the clips in her bag. It was too late to put her hair up again and she didn't want to make an issue of it. And quite apart from anything else, her hands were shaking so much that she would only make a mess of it.

Silence simmered as they waited for the lift. Inside it, they stood as far apart from each other as possible but Tess felt as if she was having to lean sideways to resist the magnetic pull that seemed to be tugging her towards Gabriel. She had the bizarre conviction that if she relaxed for an instant she would simply give in to the irresistible force that would propel her across the lift and clamp herself onto him. On her desk she had a magnetic paper clip holder. If you held the clip close enough there was a point at which it simply jumped onto the holder. It had always amused Tess before, but now she knew what the clip felt like, she didn't think she would use it any more.

The party was already in full swing by the time they got to the hotel, and Niles wore a relieved expression as he pushed his way through the crowd to welcome them. 'Now we can start the auction while everyone's still capable of writing cheques!'

A table had been set on the dais at one end of the room. Niles banged it with his gavel to get attention, and explained the rules of the auction to some jovial heckling from those who had been at the bar for some time.

'Right,' shouted Niles at last. 'We're going to begin with the promises that are up for auction. Lot one. John has promised an afternoon working in the garden. How much am I bid?'

Gabriel hardly listened. Tess had moved deliberately away from him and was standing with some of the girls he recognised from the office. He watched her covertly. There had been a moment back there in the office when he had badly wanted to kiss her, when he had known that she wouldn't have resisted if he had.

Thank God that he hadn't! Gabriel told himself. He had always stuck to women like Fionnula who knew the rules of the game and didn't pressurise him with false expectations and messy emotions. You knew where you were with Fionnula, but Tess was different. Tess was the sort of woman who expected you to mean what you said and keep any promises you made. The last thing he wanted was to get involved with a woman like her!

He fingered his mobile phone, wondering if he should confirm his decision by ringing Fionnula right now and arranging to meet her later, but the auction was well under way now, and they would all notice if he tried to slip away. He would call her later.

'Going...going...gone!' Niles brought down his gavel to a burst of applause. 'Lot ten,' he announced, well into his stride by now. 'A truly amazing opportunity! Tess Gordon has promised to cook a romantic meal for two for the highest bidder. She didn't specify whether she was one of the two but, either way, it's an offer not to be missed. So what am I bid for Tess's promise? Starting at twenty-five pounds...'

'Thirty.' someone shouted, and a brisk round of bidding ensued.

Gabriel listened with gathering frown. Most of those bidding were men, he noted darkly. Were they all hoping to have the dinner with Tess herself? He hated the idea of them bidding for her. She might end up anywhere, with anyone.

'A hundred pounds!' yelled Niles, spotting a raised hand. 'Our highest bid so far. Graham has bid a hundred pounds for Tess to cook a romantic dinner for two. Who'll give me a hundred and ten?'

Craning his neck, Gabriel spotted Graham, the director of the supplies division, looking smug. Tess, on the other hand, embarrassed by all the attention, looked as if she wished she was elsewhere.'

'Is a hundred my last offer?' Niles looked round, delighted at having raised such a sum. 'Going...going...'

'A thousand,' Gabriel heard his voice calling out.

There was a gasp. Everyone turned to stare at him in the ensuing dead silence. 'A thousand pounds,' he said again, sounding defensive.

Niles began to grin. 'I'm bid a thousand pounds for Tess's romantic dinner for two. That had better be a good dinner, Tess. Any other bids...? I didn't think so! Going, going, gone. Tess's promise sold to Mr Stearne.'

CHAPTER NINE

A HUGE cheer broke out, along with a lot of whistling and more than a few ribald comments. Mortified, Tess made her way as unobtrusively as possible to Gabriel's side while Niles was announcing that they would take a break and draw the raffle after they'd all had a chance to refill their glasses.

'That was a bit excessive, wasn't it?' she said out of the corner of her mouth.

Gabriel, wondering what madness had seized him, retreated behind a show of arrogant unconcern. 'I thought the object of the exercise was to raise money for charity?' he said, looking down his nose as if daring her to suggest that he could have had any other motive in bidding for her.

'It is, but there was no need for you to make quite such an ostentatious contribution. Everyone was having a good time until you killed the whole thing stone dead. Nobody else could possibly match that kind of money.'

'You were the one who told me to be generous,' said Gabriel, stung by her criticism. 'Obviously I had to make a bid for something, and I'm not interested in having my car washed by an accountant in a bikini.'

'At least bidding for that would have made you seem as if you had a sense of humour,' Tess retorted. 'It's not as if you've got any interest in a romantic meal either.'

'On the contrary,' he said, spotting an opportunity to convince her—or was it himself?—that when he had made that absurd bid he hadn't been thinking about her at all. 'Fionnula was saying just the other day that it would nice to have an evening in. I'm no cook, but if you could produce something special, we could make it a really romantic evening for her.'

He might as well have slapped her. Tess stiffened. Less than an hour ago, he had been thinking about kissing *her*— she had seen it in his eyes—and now she was expected to help promote his romance with Fionnula Jenkins!

'I'll do whatever you want,' she said frigidly, deciding there and then that, whatever the menu, it would be something she could do well in advance so she didn't have to watch him and Fionnula being romantic together.

Gabriel put his hand in his jacket pocket and brought out his cheque book. 'I guess I'd better hand over some money, and then perhaps I can go.'

'I don't think you'll be able to do that,' said Tess with just a trace of malice. 'Your promise hasn't been raffled off yet.'

Cursing under his breath, Gabriel went in search of Niles or one of the other members of the social committee, but when he tried to find out exactly what he had promised Niles would say only that it was coming up as the finale to the raffle. 'You can't go yet, Mr Stearne,' he protested. 'We're all relying on you.'

'What am I going to have to do?'

'We're saving it as a surprise.' Niles winked. 'But I think you'll enjoy it!'

'Is it going to take long?'

'That's up to you, sir. All I can tell you is that it's something you have to do tonight.'

Gabriel sighed and gave up. He obviously wasn't going to get any more out of them. They were all well into the drinks and were no doubt arranging something suitably humiliating for the boss from hell, as Tess called him.

He would just have to put up with it, Gabriel realised. Tess's comment about his lack of humour was rankling still. There was nothing wrong with his sense of humour, and he was quite happy to prove it to her!

The evening seemed endless. Remembering what she had said about getting to know his staff better, Gabriel made laborious conversation with various groups, most of whom seemed to be in awe of him, and tried not to notice how Tess never came near him.

After what seemed an age, with the party getting more raucous, Niles climbed back onto the dais and called for silence for the raffle. 'This is a lucky dip. You've all bought a ticket, so we're going to raffle off the remaining promises.'

There was much hilarity as the promises were solemnly read out and the winners waved their tickets. Gabriel had bought a whole book of tickets, and he was relieved that his numbers hadn't come up. He had no desire for a week's doughnut delivery to his desk, nor to be smiled at by the famously morose accounting clerk.

'And now to our final, very special, promise,' cried Niles at last. 'It's time for Mr Stearne, who's already made such a generous financial contribution this evening, to keep his promise. I know a lot of you ladies have bought tickets hoping that yours will be the one that comes up, so let's see who's going to be the lucky girl!'

Gabriel looked at Tess and raised his eyebrows, but she lifted her shoulders and shook her head to indicate that she had no idea what Niles was talking about either.

'Sir, if you'd like to come up here, please.'

They made a passage for him through to the dais. Resigned to his fate, Gabriel climbed the steps to join Niles with a forced smile.

'Mr Stearne has promised to kiss the first lady whose ticket comes out of the hat.'

There were whistles and cheers. Gabriel's expression took on a decidedly fixed quality, but he kept his smile in place. He had a sense of humour, hadn't he? He hoped Tess was watching.

'OK, girls, are you ready?'

They screamed and laughed excitedly as with a great flourish Niles drew a ticket stub out of the hat. 'Perhaps you'd like to announce the winner,' he said to Gabriel, who took the stub with a constrained smile.

'Number ninety-seven,' he read out, then his eye moved upwards to read the name scribbled above. 'Tess,' he said in a strange voice.

'Rigged!' someone called out in mock outrage, while there was another outburst of cheers and whistles.

Tess stared down at the ticket in her hand in disbelief, and then, very slowly, she lifted her eyes to meet Gabriel's gaze over the crowd.

She had been too preoccupied to pay any attention to the rumours circulating about the promises auction. Why hadn't someone told her that this was the humiliation they'd had in mind for Gabriel? She could have put a stop to it, but it was too late now. If either of them refused to go through with this ridiculous kiss, they would both look foolish, and Tess realised suddenly that she couldn't bear to do that to Gabriel. His reputation was bad enough as it was.

So she let herself be prodded forward, smiling mechanically at the merry calls of encouragement, and before she knew what was happening was climbing the steps onto the dais where Gabriel was waiting for her.

'It seems I have a promise to keep,' he said.

An expectant silence fell on the crowd watching them. Very aware of all those eyes watching his every move, Gabriel took Tess's hands. Her eyes were huge and dark, and her fingers clasped his in mute appeal. Better get this over with quickly, he thought.

Bending his head swiftly, he touched his lips to the corner of her mouth and straightened.

'Call that a kiss?' came a catcall over the whistles and laughter. 'Give her a proper kiss!'

Gabriel looked down into Tess's eyes. Moistening her

lips, she nodded almost imperceptibly. If they didn't do this properly, they would never get off this platform.

Awkwardly, he put his hands to her waist and pulled her closer. Tess's palms rested against his chest. He could feel her trembling slightly. How could he possibly kiss her with a hundred pairs of eyes staring at them?

The silence stretched agonisingly. Gabriel glanced at the crowd, and then back to Tess's golden eyes. And all at once, it was easy. His hands tightened at her waist and, as her lashes closed in sweet anticipation, his mouth came down on hers. He felt her sharp intake of breath at the touch of his lips and for an instant she tensed before something unlocked inside her and she yielded to the warmth and persuasion of his kiss.

The watching crowd was forgotten. Gabriel gathered her closer as he gave in to the temptation to kiss her the way he had so badly wanted to kiss her in office, before he had decided that he hadn't really wanted to kiss her at all. He knew now that he had just been fooling himself. Of course he had wanted to kiss her, and now that he *was* kissing her, it felt absolutely right, as if he had always known how it would be, as if she belonged in his arms.

Equally heedless of the spectators, Tess melted into him, her hands creeping up to his shoulders. Delight span her slowly, irresistibly, around, sweeping her away from reality so that she had to cling to Gabriel, intoxicated and dizzy and oblivious to anything but the warmth of his lips and the taste of his mouth and the hard security of his arms locked around her.

When he let her go, she was shaken and disorientated to find herself back on the dais, and she stared at him, shocked not by the kiss but by the suddenness with which it had ended, and hardly hearing the cheering and whistling from the delighted onlookers who had never in a million years thought that either of them would go through with it.

'Well, Tess, there are a lot of envious girls out there this evening after watching that!' Niles laughed, and a great sweep of colour burned up her cheeks as she realised just how it must have looked. She hadn't even put up a token resistance! They all must have seen how eagerly she had responded to Gabriel's kiss.

Tess didn't know where to look, nor what to do. Her heart was jerking, her nerves jumped and tingled, her mouth throbbed. Part of her wanted the dais to open up and swallow her. The other terrible, treacherous, part longed to bury back into Gabriel and to feel his arms close around her, holding her safe and protecting her from the avid stares of those waiting below.

Somehow, Tess got herself off the dais to find herself welcomed like a returning heroine. Everyone thought it was a great joke. Tess knew that she had to treat it like a joke too, to pretend that it had all been very amusing and that she had simply played along, but it was an enormous effort to steady her trembling mouth, to nod and smile and agree that, yes, Gabriel's expression when he'd heard what he had to do had been very funny.

'We rigged it,' Niles was confiding complacently to Gabriel. 'We thought that since you and Tess had been spending so much time together you would…you know…' He faltered to a stop, unsure how to interpret the look in Gabriel's eyes. 'You didn't mind, did you?' he asked belatedly.

From the dais, Gabriel looked down at Tess. She was surrounded by people who were laughing and congratulating her as if she had passed some terrible ordeal, and he remembered the slender pliancy of her body, her warmth and her softness, the sweetness of her lips.

'No, I didn't mind,' he said slowly.

Tess dressed at her most severe the next morning. After a restless night spent tossing and turning, while her mouth tingled with the imprint of Gabriel's lips and her body thumped and twitched with the memory of his hands and the hard promise they had held, she decided that her only option was to behave exactly as usual and somehow convince Gabriel that she had treated that kiss as light-heartedly as everyone else.

There was no sign of him when she got into work. Belatedly, Tess remembered that he had a meeting first thing, and didn't know whether to be relieved or disappointed that she didn't have to impress him with her dignified lack of concern right away.

The office was very quiet when he wasn't there, and she had too much time to think. Unable to concentrate on anything more complicated, Tess decided that this was the perfect opportunity to catch up on her filing. She was standing by one of the gleaming cabinets with a collection of papers and files in her hands and her back to the door when Gabriel spoke behind her, and the shock of hearing his voice a good hour earlier than she had expected him loosened her grip, sending the entire pile scattering to the floor as she swung round.

'I'm sorry,' he said in a stilted voice. ' I didn't mean to startle you.'

'It's all right. I just wasn't expecting you back yet.'

Crimson and flustered, Tess crouched to gather up the papers. Gabriel put his briefcase on her desk and bent to help her. He handed her two of the files, being very careful not to touch her, and for a moment they were linked by the buff cardboard. Their eyes caught and clung, before he broke the look and straightened abruptly.

He too had spent a restless night, and the meeting that morning had been profoundly unsatisfactory, largely because of his own inability to concentrate on what was being said. By the time he'd reached the office, he had been feeling edgy and irritable, and quite unprepared for the effect the sight of Tess would have on him.

Was still having on him.

She was standing by her desk, making a big deal of tidying the pile of papers they had gathered. Her hair was up, as usual, and he could see the nape of her neck, so soft and vulnerable and alluring. Gabriel had a terrible urge to press his lips to it.

What would she do if he did? Would she recoil in horror? Or would she lean back into him with a slow shiver of response, smiling and tilting her head so that he could kiss his way down her throat?

Appalled at the wayward drift of his imagination, Gabriel swallowed hard and practically snatched his briefcase from the desk. 'When you've finished sorting those out, perhaps you could come into my office?' he said gruffly.

Tess thought she had herself well under control by the time she had found her notebook and knocked on his door. 'You wanted me?' she said without thinking and then blushed like a fool, her precious poise slipping disastrously as she heard the *double entendre* in her words.

Gabriel looked up from his computer, his eyes piercingly light and alert, and he let the silence beat for a second or two, just long enough to let her know that he had heard it too.

'Yes, I did,' he agreed.

He dictated a couple of letters and asked her to make various arrangements which Tess noted, proud of the fact that her hands were absolutely steady. Well, quite steady, anyway.

Then he fell silent, shifting the papers around on his desk. 'About last night,' he said at last, and Tess stiffened. It wasn't fair of him to bring last night up, just when she had let herself believe that he wasn't going to mention it.

'What about it?' she said with a hostile look.

'Do you know who was responsible for setting us up like that?'

Tess had her strong suspicions but she shook her head. 'No, but I don't think you should make an issue of it,' she said as coolly as she could. 'It was meant to be a bit of fun, that's all.'

'I didn't think it was fun,' said Gabriel and held her eyes deliberately. 'Did you?'

The memory of the kiss blazed between them. It had been amazing, overwhelming, terrifying in its intensity, but *fun*? No, not fun.

Her gaze slid away from his. 'I think you'll find that it was a good thing for you to have done,' she said, not answering him directly. 'You showed everyone that you're prepared to have a laugh and let yourself be the butt of a joke. That will have done more for your relations with the staff here than a hundred memos.'

'And that makes it all right, does it?'

She fiddled with her pen. 'I know it was…thoughtless…and embarrassing…' she said, choosing her words with care, 'but it's too late to change what happened now. You might as well make the best of it.'

'What about you?' Gabriel was unreasonably annoyed by Tess's calmly sensible attitude. Obviously *she* hadn't spent the night tossing and turning and wondering what it would have been like if they hadn't been kissing in front of a roomful of people, if they'd been on their own, with no one to laugh or to cheer, with no reason to stop…

'It wasn't just me up there making an exhibition of myself. They set you up, too.'

'Oh, well…' Tess managed a careless shrug. 'Judging by the reaction I got afterwards, it obviously did wonders for my image too. They've always thought of me as a bit prim and proper, I think. That's probably why they chose me.'

Seeing that Gabriel looked unconvinced, she leant forward in her chair. 'It was all very silly, I agree,' she said, trying her best to make light of it, 'but it wasn't such a terrible experience, was it?' she added bravely.

Gabriel didn't answer. He just looked at her, remembering the feel of her in his arms. He wished he could dismiss it as casually as she seemed to be able to. 'You're taking it all very well,' he commented in a hard voice.

'I don't see any point in making a fuss,' said Tess lightly. 'It wasn't as if it meant anything. It was just a kiss.'

Yes, all right, he'd got the point that it hadn't meant anything to her, thought Gabriel savagely.

'I think we should forget the whole incident,' she was continuing, ignoring the way his jaw was working. 'It was all for a good cause. They raised a lot of money through the auction.' Tess was very proud of her nonchalant manner. 'Talking of which, when would you like me to keep my promise?'

He frowned. 'What promise?'

'To cook you a romantic dinner for two.'

'Oh,' he said flatly, 'that promise.'

'You paid a lot of money for it,' she reminded him.

He had, Gabriel remembered. Well, it was time to reassure Tess that he wasn't taking that kiss any more seriously than she was.

'I'll see if Fionnula is free this weekend,' he said. 'Shall we say Saturday night?'

Tess flashed a brittle smile as she got to her feet. 'Saturday would be fine,' she said.

'I can't see what I'm doing,' Gabriel complained, looking up from the report he was trying to read. Tess had put off the overhead lights and was setting the blinds to slide across the window with a faint electronic hum.

'You're not supposed to be able to read,' she told him, switching on a table lamp. 'A romantic meal is all about atmosphere.'

That was what he had paid for, and that was what he was going to get, she had vowed to herself.

Returning to the kitchen, she reappeared a few moments later with some flowers and candles, which she set at strategic points around the room. She would light them just before she left, so that they would be flickering romantically when Fionnula arrived. Some perverse instinct had made Tess determined to create the ultimate romantic meal for them both.

'Now all you need is music,' she said, surveying the room with satisfaction when she had finished.

'I haven't got any music,' said Gabriel, who had been watching her as she'd been moving around, graceful in spite of the apron tied over the soft skirt and less than glamorous baggy cardigan she wore. She hadn't really done much to the room, but somehow the whole atmosphere of the apartment had changed. It seemed warmer, softer, more welcoming. Or was it just her presence that had made it that way?

'I've brought a CD with me,' said Tess, organised as ever. 'I'll leave it here for tonight, and collect it when I pick up the rest of my stuff.' She glanced at Gabriel. 'Come into the kitchen. I'll show you what you have to do.'

He followed her reluctantly. 'These are your starters,' she said, gesturing to the plates of fresh asparagus that she had prepared, 'and your puddings are in the fridge.' She opened the door to show him two heart-shaped chocolate desserts. 'There's champagne chilling in there, too. And the chicken just needs to be reheated when you're ready for it.'

'But you'll be here to do that, won't you?' said Gabriel, eyeing the array of dishes apprehensively.

'Me?' Tess was determinedly brisk, the way she had been ever since she had arrived to make the last minute preparations. 'Of course not! I don't think Fionnula would find it very romantic with me lurking around in the background,' she added dryly. 'I'll make sure I go before she arrives. What time did you tell her?'

'Eight o'clock,' he said, conscious of a certain lack of enthusiasm in his voice.

Tess checked her watch. It was twenty past seven. 'That'll just give me time to do the salad.'

Gabriel looked around him, appalled by all the trouble that she had taken to make it a special evening, and even more by the realisation that he was dreading it. How the hell had he got himself into this situation?

'Is there anything I can do?' he asked awkwardly.

'I think you should change, so that you're ready when Fionnula arrives.'

She seemed very keen to promote his relationship with Fionnula, thought Gabriel glumly as he stood under the shower. *He* was the one who ought to be keen. Fionnula was beautiful, uninhibited and too ambitious to be interested in any kind of emotional commitment. She was perfect.

So why was he standing here thinking about Tess in her worn cardigan, about the curve of her jaw and the line of her throat?

'Does your romantic atmosphere call for a tie?' he asked her as he went back into the kitchen, effectively disguising his own confusion beneath an air of ironic resignation. 'Or can I wear this shirt on its own?'

Tess turned from the cooker, where she was tasting the sauce on a wooden spoon. Gabriel had on his most sardonic expression. His hair was still wet from the shower, and he was wearing a pale yellow shirt that intensified his dark features and made the lightness of his eyes even more startling. He looked devastating, Tess thought involuntarily, and her heart, which she had kept so firmly under control until now, spoilt everything by lurching into her throat at the sight of him.

'I think you're all right as you are,' she said, horrified to hear the betraying croak in her voice. She swallowed. 'You look...very nice.'

'Tess,' said Gabriel on an impulse, and then stopped.

'What?'

Yes, *what*? Gabriel asked himself. What had he been going to say? Tess, I can't stop thinking about you? Tess, let me untie your apron and slide that cardigan from your shoulders? Tess, let me kiss you again?

Fionnula would be arriving any minute. 'Oh...nothing,' he said.

There was a constrained silence. It stretched between them, so taut that when Gabriel's mobile phone rang, they both jerked back as if an elastic band pulling them together had snapped.

Gabriel answered it in the living area. Tess couldn't hear what he was saying but, judging by the briefness of his murmured replies, it wasn't a particularly friendly call. And, indeed, when eventually he reappeared his face was grim and his mouth set in a angry line. 'That was Fionnula,' he said baldly. 'She's not coming.'

'Not coming?' Tess echoed in disbelief. 'Why not?'

'Something's come up.'

Fionnula had been invited to fill in on a live panel show at the last minute, she had told him. She'd been sure that he would understand that she couldn't turn down any chance of exposure. If she wanted to stay successful, she had to stay in the public eye. 'It's a bore, darling, I know, but there it is.'

'But I told you that tonight was different,' Gabriel protested. 'Tess has gone to a lot of trouble to cook a special meal for us.'

'Tess?' Fionnula's voice dropped several degrees.

'Yes, you've met her,' he said impatiently. 'She's my assistant.'

'Oh, the one you couldn't keep your eyes off in the restaurant?'

'Yes...no!' He corrected himself hastily.

'She must be a very special assistant if she cooks as well as she does everything else for you,' said Fionnula, dripping sarcasm. 'No wonder you're in love with her. You ought to marry her, darling, and save yourself a salary.'

'Of course I'm not in love with her.' Gritting his teeth, Gabriel tried to explain the promises auction. 'The whole point of her being here is to make it a special evening for you,' he said.

'It wouldn't be very special for me with you spending your whole time trying not to look at your secretary. I had enough of that the other night.'

'Don't be ridiculous!' snapped Gabriel, his temper fraying. 'Look, you've got plenty of work at the moment. You don't have to be on every cheap game show that calls you up at the last minute.'

He drew a breath and made himself sound calm and reasonable. 'Why don't you tell them no for once, and come round here?' he coaxed her, only to spoil everything by adding, 'Otherwise Tess will have gone to all this effort for nothing. The food won't keep until tomorrow, and she's already given up her evening to get everything ready for you.'

'Oh, well, we can't have your precious PA put out, can we?' said Fionnula vindictively. 'If you're that bothered about it, I suggest you share your special meal with her. Frankly, I've got more interesting things to do!' And she slammed the phone down.

Gabriel was furious. He felt a fool telling Tess that Fionnula wasn't coming after all.

'She had to work,' he said uncomfortably. 'I'm sorry.'

Tess looked around the kitchen where everything was set out ready to be served or heated up. 'This will all be wasted,' she said in dismay. 'Is there any one else you can ask to come over?'

Gabriel looked at her with a slight frown. 'You're in love with her,' Fionnula had said. Absurd! He didn't fall in love with anyone, let alone someone like Tess. Still in her apron, she was holding a wooden spoon and looking worried. There was a smudge of flour on her cheek. She looked ordinary, unthreatening, not at all the kind of person who could turn his life upside down.

Gabriel's expression relaxed slightly. Of course he wasn't in love with her. That had just been Fionnula being spiteful. He would prove it.

'Well,' he said slowly, 'there's you.'

'*Me?*'

'Did you have any other plans for this evening?'

'No,' admitted Tess after a moment.

'Then, why not stay and share the meal with me? You said yourself that it won't keep, and I can't eat it all myself. We may as well make the most of it after all the trouble you've taken.'

Tess hesitated. 'I don't know…'

'It's too short notice to ask anyone else.' Gabriel was surprised by how much he suddenly wanted her to stay. 'If you won't keep me company, I'll be stuck here all on my own with the candles and the bottle of champagne, and that won't be very romantic, will it?'

'No, I suppose not, but—'

'I paid for a romantic meal for two,' he reminded her unfairly. 'You were the one who made the promise, so the least you can do is ensure that's what I get.'

Tess could feel herself weakening. 'I've booked a taxi for ten to eight,' she told him.

'Ring and change it to later.'

Helplessly, she looked down at her old cardigan, worn skirt and comfortable shoes. 'I'm not really dressed for a special meal…'

'You look fine to me,' said Gabriel firmly. 'All you need is to take off that apron.'

Going over to her, he took the wooden spoon from her hand. 'It's not like you to dither, Tess,' he told her as he turned her around, untied the apron and pulled it over her head. Casting an eye around, he spotted her handbag and thrust it into her arms. 'You go and freshen up,' he ordered her. 'I'll ring the cab company.'

Tess gave in. Her stomach churned with a mixture of apprehension and anticipation and her hands shook slightly as she washed her face and hands. At least she had her make-up bag with her. By the time she had taken off her cardigan to reveal a close-fitting top with a scoop neck, had brushed out her hair and had put on some lipstick, she was able to face the situation with a bit more confidence.

It didn't stop her feeling ridiculously shy when she came face to face with Gabriel again. He was coming out of the kitchen with the champagne bottle in one hand and two flutes in the other, and they both stopped dead at the same time.

'If you're ready,' said Gabriel lightly after a moment, 'let's start our romantic evening. I've got the champagne and the glasses. What else do we need?'

'Candlelight.' Entering into the spirit of things, Tess found some matches and lit the candles until the room was bathed in a soft, flickering glow. She stood back to admire the effect. 'Perfect,' she said with a smile. There was no need to take this seriously, after all. They were only playing at it.

She sat down on the big, squashy sofa and kicked off her shoes so that she could curl her legs beneath her. Gabriel eased the cork expertly out of the bottle and poured champagne into the flutes with a satisfying fizz. Handing one to Tess, he sat down beside her and raised his glass.

'What shall we drink to?'

Tess looked at the bubbles drifting in her glass and tried not to think about how close he was. 'To keeping our promises?' she suggested.

'To promises,' agreed Gabriel, and they chinked glasses solemnly.

There was a silence while both thought about the promise he had kept, about the way they had kissed. Tess could feel memory tightening the air around them and was gripped by sudden panic. This was madness! She should never have agreed to stay. She should have taken her bag and walked away and left Gabriel with his dinner.

Her eyes skittered frantically around the room, desperate for something to hold their attention, but it was no use. They were being dragged irresistibly back to Gabriel, to his hands, to his throat, to his mouth... Oh, God, his *mouth*...

Tess drew in a sharp breath as the memory of how it had felt against her own clawed at the base of her spine, and she wrenched her gaze away, only to find herself looking deep into Gabriel's disquietingly light eyes. They held an expression Tess couldn't identify, but which made her heart shift suddenly in her chest, and she put her glass down on the coffee table with an uncertain click.

'I—I'd better see what's happening in the kitchen,' she said breathlessly.

The lights there were bright and reassuring. To her horror, when she checked the sauce, Tess realised that her hands were shaking. She had been doing so well, too. She had carried off the awkwardness of the situation, had pretended that the idea of being alone with Gabriel didn't bother her in the least, only to spoil everything by talking about the promises they had made and looking deep into his eyes.

She wouldn't do that again, Tess told herself. There was no need for her to be looking at him at all, let alone wondering what that light in his eyes meant or why it should suddenly be so hard to breathe. There was no need for her to be excruciatingly aware of him as a man, of the stern angles of his face and the tantalising texture of his skin and the solid, masculine strength of his body. No need to imagine sliding across the sofa and unbuttoning his shirt.

No need at all.

She would stick to strictly impersonal subjects for rest of evening, Tess decided firmly. She was just here to eat up the food, and she had better not forget it.

So she flashed Gabriel a bright smile when she picked up her glass and rejoined him on the sofa, and steered the conversation into what she hoped were determinedly neutral channels.

Only it didn't quite work like that. They talked about work for a while but, once they got onto personalities, they ended inevitably at the promises auction where they had kissed, so they switched to Harry. A baby ought to be a safe enough subject, thought Tess, and it was fine until they got onto remembering their first ham-fisted attempts to feed him and change him, which made them laugh, at which point Harry didn't seem such a good topic of conversation either.

They tried talking about their respective brothers, about their childhoods, about places they had been and books they had read and movies they had seen. They even tried politics. None of them were runners.

By the time the main course was over, their inspiration was exhausted. They were reduced to bursts of feverish conversation that withered and died after a few exchanges, leaving them racking their brains desperately for some new and inexhaustible subject that would have no connection to anything that they had in common, a subject that they could discuss like two sensible people without looking at each other and realising that they were alone in the candlelight and all it would take was for one of them to reach out a hand and they would be touching.

Tess hardly tasted a mouthful of the food she had spent so long preparing. The more she reminded herself that this should have been Fionnula's evening, the more she noticed how the candlelight threw the hard, exciting lines of Gabriel's face into relief, the more her eyes clung to his hands, to his mouth, to the pulse beating below his ear.

She wanted him to kiss her again.

The breath dried in Tess's throat as she admitted the truth to herself. She wanted him to pull her against him. She wanted him to twist his fingers in her hair and bring his mouth down hard on hers. And she wanted to kiss him back, to tug the shirt from his trousers and run her hands over his chest. She wanted—

Stop it! Stop it!

Tess pushed her plate aside. She had hardly touched the rich chocolate mousse that had taken her so long to make in its pretty heart shape. 'My taxi will be here soon,' she croaked. 'I should think about clearing up.'

'Forget clearing up,' said Gabriel softly. 'This is supposed to be a romantic dinner, and romantic dinners don't usually end with washing up, do they?'

Very slowly, Tess's eyes lifted to meet his, and she knew she was lost.

'No,' she said. 'They don't.'

CHAPTER TEN

GABRIEL'S chair scraped across the polished wooden floor as he stood up. 'I think it would be a good idea if we moved somewhere more comfortable, don't you?'

Tess didn't think it was a good idea at all. She thought it was a very bad idea, even a dangerous idea, but she could hardly insist on staying where she was. Nursing the end of her wine, she perched on the edge of the sofa, turning the glass nervously between her fingers and gazing with a kind of desperation at the guttering candles in front of her, to stop her eyes crawling sideways to Gabriel. He was lounging on the sofa beside her, close, but not touching. Not quite.

'What's happened to the music?' he said, breaking the strumming silence. He rose and set the CD to play again. Tess had brought a compilation of love songs from the fifties and sixties, slow, smoochy numbers that Gabriel hadn't heard for years but which were instantly familiar.

He turned back to Tess sitting tensely on the sofa. 'Come on,' he said abruptly. 'Let's dance.'

'Oh, no, I—'

'You must,' he said, breaking into her instinctive protest. 'It won't be a romantic evening without dancing.'

'No, really, I'm a hopeless dancer,' said Tess, shrinking back into the cushions, but Gabriel was already reaching down to take the wine glass from her nerveless grasp and setting it on the table.

'I don't believe you,' he said and pulled her to her feet. 'You're good at everything else.'

She wasn't good at keeping her distance, thought Tess. She wasn't any good at resisting him. She wasn't good at

168

emembering all the reasons why she shouldn't fall in love
with him.

'Not everything,' she said a little unsteadily.

Gabriel clasped her hand against his shoulder, and put
a strong arm around her waist to draw her towards him.
'You don't need to be good at dancing, anyway,' he said,
glancing down at her averted face. 'You just need to let
me hold you.'

Pulling her closer, he trod on her foot as he swung her
ound. 'See?' he murmured in her ear. 'I can't dance either.
We'll have to stand here and sway.'

This is crazy, thought Tess frantically. She would never
be able to go back to being his PA after this. How could
she take memos and keep his diary and book restaurants
for him when she knew how it felt to be held against him
ike this? But it was too late to think about that now. She
should have gone while she'd had the chance. The whole
evening had been a terrible mistake.

Except it hadn't felt like a mistake, and it didn't now.
It felt like the only place she wanted to be, cocooned in
warmth and candlelight with Gabriel, isolated from the rest
of the world by this bubble of enchantment. With his arm
around her and his hand clasping hers, it was easy to forget
that come Monday she would have to walk into the office
and pretend that this had never happened. The future didn't
exist. There was only now, and the two of them alone
together with the words of the old love songs swirling
around them.

His fingers were warm around hers, holding her tightly
while his other hand smoothed slowly up and down her
spine. Boneless and dizzy with desire, Tess was powerless
to stop herself leaning into him and closing her eyes.

Gabriel felt her quivering resistance eke away. He gathered her closer, turning his face into her silky hair and
breathing in her fragrance. 'Now, this is romantic, isn't
t?' he said, his voice very deep and low.

She nodded, unable to speak.

'Of course, if we were going to be really romantic, i' wouldn't be enough to dance like this. I'd have to kiss you, wouldn't I?'

A tremor ran through her. 'If this was real,' she managed with difficulty, 'but it's not real. We're just pretending.'

'Are we?' Gabriel bent his head and kissed the lobe of her ear. 'It feels real to me,' he breathed, kissing his way along her jaw and smiling as he felt Tess shudder with pleasure.

'I don't think this is…sensible,' she whispered.

'No, it isn't,' he murmured against her throat. 'It's no' sensible at all. But it's romance, it's here and now. It's what you promised and what I paid for. And right now, I don't want to be sensible, do you?'

Releasing Tess's hand, he pushed her hair gently away from her face and cupped her cheek with his palm, tilting her chin so that she was looking up at him.

'Do you?' he asked softly again.

Very slowly, Tess shook her head, and saw a blaze of expression in his eyes before his mouth found hers at last and the terrible tension of the evening exploded into hunger and delight and intense, rocketing excitement. Succumbing to the rush of sensation, she wound her arms around Gabriel's neck and clung to him, kissing him back with a kind of desperation.

After waiting so long, she couldn't hold him tightly enough, couldn't kiss him deeply enough. It was bliss to be able to run her hands over his powerful shoulders, to give herself up to the taste and touch and the feel of him.

Without being aware of how it happened, Tess found herself back on the sofa, with Gabriel kissing his way down her throat, murmuring endearments against her skin. She arched beneath him and tangled her fingers in his hair and, when his hand slid beneath her top, she gasped at the feel of flesh against flesh, beyond remembering what sensible meant, beyond thinking at all, lost in a tumbling tide of desire.

A harsh buzzing sound was jarring the gentle melody from the CD player, filtering insistently through the sound of their breathing. Gabriel heard it first and he lifted his head with a frown.

'That'll be my taxi,' said Tess shakily, belatedly recognising the buzz of the intercom.

She tried to sit up but Gabriel kept her pinned beneath him. 'Stay,' he urged her. 'I'll tell him to go.'

But that would mean him going all the way down to the entrance to pay off the cab. The spell would be broken. Perhaps it already was, thought Tess sadly.

'No—I—I'd better go.'

'Are you sure?'

For a moment, she wavered, biting her lip. Her body clamoured to let him persuade her to stay right where she was, but her head, annoyed at being so comprehensively ignored up till then, reminded her sternly of all the reasons why that would be a bad idea. A very bad idea.

'I'm sure,' she said huskily.

Gabriel levered himself abruptly off her and went over to the intercom as the cab driver leant impatiently on the buzzer again. 'Five minutes,' he said curtly into the speaker, and turned back to Tess, who was gathering her things together with trembling hands.

She glanced at the table where they had left their plates and glasses what seemed like a lifetime ago. 'What about all this?' she said in a brave attempt to sound normal.

'Leave it. I'll sort it out,' said Gabriel with a twisted smile. 'I won't have anything else to do.'

At the door, he kissed her once, hard. 'I wish you'd stay,' he said.

'I…can't,' said Tess, weak-kneed and clutching desperately at her resolution.

'Coward,' he said softly.

'Maybe I am.' She forced a smile. 'But I'm a sensible coward.'

Gabriel ran a finger down her cheek. 'You weren't being sensible a few minutes ago.'

'I know,' she said, her skin seared with his touch. 'I got a bit carried away with the romantic atmosphere.' Drawing a breath, she made herself look directly at him. 'I think we should agree to forget this evening.'

There was a pause. Gabriel's hand fell to his side. 'Is that really what you want?' he said in disbelief.

'Yes.' Tess put up her chin, not sure whether she was defying him or the voice inside her that was shouting, No. No! That's not what I want at all.

'Everything will look different in the morning,' she said, keeping her voice steady with an effort. 'And on Monday I'm going to have to walk into the office and be your secretary again. I can only do that if we both pretend this never happened.'

Gabriel looked at her for a long moment before giving a curt nod. 'All right,' he said, swallowing the bitterness of his disappointment. Because what else could he say? He knew how much Tess needed her job, and he needed her. He couldn't be responsible for putting her in an impossible situation.

He opened the door reluctantly. 'We'll pretend nothing happened if that's what you want. I won't ring you and I won't discuss it, but if you change your mind about tonight, come back. I'll be here.'

Tess sat rigidly upright in the back of the cab, staring unseeingly out at the dark London streets while the memory of Gabriel's kisses raged through her. Leaving had been the only sensible thing to do, Tess knew that. She knew that she had done the right thing. But it had felt so right in his arms, so real. Much more real than this taxi with its ticking meter and its strange taxi smell and its thankfully morose driver.

Coward, Gabriel had called her, and he was right. She was afraid of falling in love with him, afraid of getting hurt the way Oliver had hurt her before. But Gabriel wasn't Oliver. He hadn't made her any promises nor told her any lies. He had offered her a night, no more. He had offered her the here and now, with no thought of tomorrow, just his lips and his hands and the feel of his body, and she had been too much of a coward to admit that was enough.

'Come back,' he had said. 'I'll be here.'

The taxi was turning into her street when Tess leant forward and spoke to the driver. 'I've changed my mind. Can you take me back?'

Grumbling, the driver turned the car round and retraced their route across the bridge and back through the heart of London to draw up across the road from Gabriel's apartment. Tess's fingers were shaking as she searched in her purse for the money to pay him. At last she located a couple of notes, and sat forward to pass them over to the driver but, even as he took them with a martyred sigh, she caught sight of someone approaching the front door.

Red hair glowed in the harsh security light as the figure pressed the intercom and waited confidently for the door to be released.

Fionnula.

Tess froze with her hand outstretched. Had Fionnula decided to make up for her earlier rejection of Gabriel? A worse thought slid insidiously into her mind. Had Gabriel rung her as soon as he'd realised that *she* wasn't going to change her mind and send the taxi away? Surely even he couldn't casually hope to substitute one woman for another within an hour?

He wouldn't let Fionnula in, Tess told herself. He couldn't let her in.

But he did let her in.

Tess watched numbly as Fionnula pushed open the door and disappeared inside. She would take the lift up to his floor and Gabriel would be waiting for her. Would he kiss Fionnula against the door? Would they sink onto the sofa together? Or would they go straight to bed?

Tess squeezed her eyes shut against the thought. It was her own fault. She should have stayed while she'd had the chance.

Except that now she knew that leaving had been the right thing to do, after all. It was all very well telling herself that a night would have been enough, but of course it wouldn't have been. She would have had to face the fact that she was in love with him, and what happiness could there be with a man like Gabriel, who didn't want compromise and didn't want commitment, who only wanted love to last long enough?

'Do you want your change or not?'

The taxi driver's weary demand made Tess open her eyes. He was holding out a handful of coins, and watching her with a mixture of suspicion and concern.

'I'm sorry,' she said bleakly. 'I've made a mistake. I want to go home.'

'Good morning, Tess.'

'Good morning.'

Gabriel eyed her with resentment. How could she sit there so self-possessed? When she had told him that she wanted to forget Saturday evening, he hadn't thought that she would really be able to do it. Her eyes hadn't so much as flickered when he'd come in. It was as if she had wiped the whole incident for her mind.

If only he had been able to do the same.

After she had gone, he had blown out the candles very deliberately. He'd switched off the music and had cleared up the debris from the meal, working with a ferocious concentration as if trying to erase Tess's presence from his apartment. He had wanted her to stay too badly. Things had been going too far, too fast. Gabriel had known that they had been in danger of getting complicated. Worse, he had been in danger of getting involved.

No, it was just as well Tess had gone when she had.

That didn't stop him leaping for the intercom when the sound of the buzzer ripped through the empty apartment. She had come back after all!

'Come on up,' he had said, and afterwards he had cringed when he'd remembered the ridiculous smile that had spread over his face. 'I'll meet you at the lift.'

Impatiently, he'd waited for the doors to slide open. 'I'm so glad you've come—' he'd begun and had then stopped, because it hadn't been Tess who'd stepped smiling seductively out of the lift. It had been Fionnula.

Gabriel shuddered at the memory of the scene that had followed. If anything had told him how he felt about Tess, it had been the bitterness of his disappointment. It had been some time before he'd heard a word Fionnula had been saying. All he'd been able to take in had been the fact that Tess hadn't come back after all.

He'd spent most of Sunday looking at the phone. Gabriel had lost count of the number of times he'd picked it up and begun to dial her number before cutting the connection. He had said that he wouldn't call her. Tess could have stayed if she had wanted to, and he wasn't going to humiliate himself by crawling after her.

If she wanted to pretend that nothing had happened, that was fine by him. There was no way Gabriel was going to let her guess the turmoil raging inside him. He had never felt like this before, and he didn't like it.

Things might have been different if Tess had shown any sign of confusion when she'd seen him that morning, if she had given the slightest hint that she even remembered kissing him but, as it was, Gabriel decided there and then that he had to get away for a while. It was all very well for Tess to say that they should just forget what had happened, but how could he forget when she was right there every day?

Gabriel didn't care if it looked as if he was running away. He had been neglecting his offices in the States, and it was high time he paid them some attention. There would be so much to do over there that he would have no time to think about Tess.

That was what he told himself, anyway.

'I want you to get me a seat on this afternoon's flight to New York,' he told her.

He watched her closely to see if he could detect any sign of disappointment in her face, but she only asked calmly when he would be coming back.

'I haven't decided yet,' he said tetchily. 'Get me an open return.'

'What about your meetings this week?'

'Reschedule them.'

'Very well.' Tess looked up at him over the top of her spectacles. 'Do you expect to be gone more than a week?'

'Possibly,' said Gabriel. 'Why?' He tensed. Was she going to say that she would miss him?

She hesitated. 'I think I should tell you that I will be handing in my resignation later today. I'll work out a month's notice, of course, but you might like to set arrangements for finding a replacement in train before you go.'

It was as if she had kicked him in the stomach. Winded, shocked, Gabriel stared at her. 'You're leaving?' he echoed numbly.

Tess swallowed. 'Yes.'

'Is it because of what happened on Saturday?' He hadn't meant to mention it, had been determined not to, in fact, but the question was out before he could stop it.

'No,' she said, but her eyes didn't quite meet his. 'We agreed that wasn't important.'

She might have agreed it, Gabriel thought bitterly. His own feelings apparently didn't matter.

'Then why?' he asked in a hard voice.

'I've been offered another job,' she told him. 'A good job. I'm going to be office manager. I've been wanting to get away from a secretarial role for some time, and this is the perfect opportunity for me to develop my career.'

Gabriel's jaw worked furiously. If she didn't want to be a secretary any more, there wasn't much he could offer her as an inducement to stay, was there? 'I suppose you'll want a reference before I go?' he bit out.

'That won't be necessary,' said Tess composedly. 'Steve knows me well enough.'

'Steve? Steve Robinson?' Gabriel was very white about the mouth. 'Is that who you're going to work for?'

'Yes.'

'I see.' He was gripped by such a murderous rage that he could hardly speak. She was going, leaving him for Steve Robinson! 'Well, I suppose I should congratulate you.' He managed to get the words out somehow.

'Thank you.'

Gabriel turned blindly for his office. 'You'd better get onto personnel. Tell them to advertise the post right away. I want someone suitable to start as soon as possible.'

Tess looked after him, her eyes stinging with the tears she had kept so tightly under control while she'd been talking to him. Was that all she meant to Gabriel? A suitable secretary who could be replaced if necessary, the same way he had replaced her with Fionnula on Saturday?

She was glad he was going away. It would make it much easier to get through the next four weeks. After making her decision on Sunday, she had called Steve right away, but deep down she knew that it was already too late. She was in love with Gabriel, and nothing she could do would change that now, but at least the new job gave her the chance to walk away from him with her pride intact. That was something.

Not much, but something.

Six weeks later, buffeted by vicious gusts of wind and rain, Tess wrestled with her umbrella in the meagre shelter of the bus stop before giving up the unequal struggle and deciding that she would just have to get wet. Turning up her collar, she set off to walk home, her shoulders hunched against the rain. It was dark and cold and miserable. The only thing to be said about the weather, Tess thought bleakly, was that it matched her mood perfectly.

She had been office manager for two weeks now. Her office was nice, the people were friendly, and the job was busy and stimulating. At last she had the challenge she had thought she'd wanted.

Except that the challenge wasn't in running a strange office. The challenge was forgetting Gabriel. Tess had hoped that it would be easier by now, but the less she saw him the worse it got.

The last few weeks at SpaceWorks had been agony. In the end, Gabriel had stayed in the States for nearly three weeks, and he'd only been back for a day to approve the choice of his new PA before setting off for Frankfurt. Tess didn't know whether to be glad or sorry that he had missed her leaving party. He had sent her an e-mail, thanking her for her help and wishing her success in her new job, but the message had been so impersonal that Tess had wanted to cry when she'd read it. He had sent her some flowers, too, but they didn't mean anything. One of the other secretaries had confided that Gabriel had asked her to arrange them while he'd been away.

Time and again, Tess told herself that she had made the right decision, but it didn't ease the dull ache in her heart that sharpened like the grinding of knives whenever she remembered the time she had spent with Gabriel—which was every unoccupied moment. She couldn't think about anything else. Over and over, she relived the feel of his arms around her, his lips on hers.

At night, she lay in bed and tortured herself by imagining how different things might have been if Gabriel had persuaded her to stay that evening in his apartment. They would have woken up together, the way they had done once before, but this time he wouldn't have frozen in horror when he realised just who he was kissing awake. They could have spent Sunday together, a long, lazy, luxurious day making love, could have gone into the office together on Monday.

And then what? Tess's dreams always stopped at this point. She couldn't imagine calmly going back to typing memos and organising meetings and booking tables for him at Cupiditas. A night, maybe two, was all she would have had. Why would he have wanted her for longer than that, when he had someone like Fionnula, who was so much more beautiful in the cold light of day, and who didn't demand anything more than he was prepared to give?

No, it would have been impossible, Tess reminded herself drearily. She had been right to leave. She just hadn't thought it would be so hard not even seeing him.

Head down, she hurried down her street while the wind tore her hair out its clips and the rain lashed against her face. Her eyes were screwed up against the wet, and it wasn't until she pushed open the gate that she realised that someone was waiting for her on her doorstep.

It was Gabriel.

The sight of him stopped the breath in Tess's throat and drove all feeling from her like a blow. He was hunched, like her, against the rain, dark hair plastered to his head and his face dripping. She stared at him, hardly daring to believe that he was real and not some mirage conjured up by her desperate longing.

'Tess,' he said, as if his throat hurt him, and the sound of his voice sent sensation whooshing back in a dizzying rush to Tess's head and to her heart.

'Wh-what are you doing here?' she croaked.

'Waiting for you.'

'In the rain?' she asked, still dazed.

'I wanted to see you,' he said. 'I knew you'd come home eventually.'

Tess hardly heard him. She couldn't get beyond the wonderful, glorious fact that he was there, right there, waiting for her.

Belatedly, she realised the rain was streaming down his face, and puddling around their feet as they stood there. 'You'd better come in,' she said.

Gabriel stood back while she unlocked the front door. She seemed to have lost all control of her hands, and she fumbled with the key, almost dropping it several times. It took ages to get it into the lock, but at last she got the door open and switched on the light.

He stepped into the hall behind her. Under the harsh electric glare, Tess saw for the first time that he was look-ing tired and drawn. 'I'll take your coat,' she said awk-wardly, and then exclaimed as she felt how heavy it was. 'It's sodden!'

'I was standing out there for nearly two hours,' said Gabriel. 'I thought you would be back before now.'

'I was working late.'

'On a Friday night?'

Without him, there had been nothing to come home to, Tess remembered. She hadn't known that he would be there, waiting for her in the rain.

'Oh, well…you know…' Awkwardly, she opened the sitting room door. 'Come and sit down.'

Gabriel sat in the armchair, leaning forward, wiping the rain from his face with the flat of his hands. Tess longed to be able to do it for him, to touch him, to feel the warmth of his skin, to convince herself that this was real, that he was really there. Instead, she fidgeted around the sitting room, pulling the curtains, putting on the lamps, kneeling to fiddle with the gas fire.

It was Gabriel who broke the silence. 'I saw Harry yesterday,' he said, sounding as ill at ease as Tess felt, and she looked up sharply. She had kept in touch with Leanne but she hadn't heard from her for a while.

'He's all right, isn't he?' she asked in concern.

'He's fine. Greg's over,' Gabriel explained. 'I took him to meet his son.'

'Oh.' Tess looked a little doubtful. 'How did that go?'

'OK, I think. Greg was on his best behaviour. He asked Leanne to marry him—in a burst of chivalry, I guess—but she said that she'd rather just be friends. Leanne's no fool,' he went on. 'She knows how unreliable Greg would be as a husband and, now that she's finally accepted an allowance, she's got some financial security. She won't need to leave Harry again.'

'I'm glad about the allowance,' said Tess. 'Is Greg paying that?'

'Leanne thinks he is,' Gabriel answered obliquely.

Tess nodded slowly, appreciating the situation. There was a lot you could say about Gabriel, but never that he wasn't generous. 'That's good.'

After the burst of conversation, another strained silence fell, broken only by the hiss and flicker of the gas flames.

'Is that what you wanted to see me about?' she asked at last.

Gabriel ran a finger around his collar. 'No... Well, partly, I guess... I thought you would want to know about Harry and—but no, it wasn't that.' He admitted the truth abruptly, 'I just wanted to see you.'

He swallowed. 'The thing is,' he said, 'I miss you.'

'You've only had your new PA for two weeks,' said

Tess with difficulty. 'It's bound to take a little time to get used to her.'

'No, you don't understand. I miss *you*.' He stopped, hearing the inadequacy of his words, but all he could think of was to try them again a different way. 'I *miss* you.'

Still kneeling by the fire, Tess heard the slow slam of her heart against her ribs. She couldn't move, couldn't speak. She could only stare at Gabriel with dark, dazed eyes while hope trickled tentatively along her veins.

'That's why I came.' Now that he had started, Gabriel couldn't stop. 'I had to tell you that there hasn't been a day since you left when I haven't missed you.' His voice deepened. 'There hasn't been a day since we kissed when I haven't wanted you.

'I told myself that I would forget you in the States, but I couldn't. I couldn't stop remembering, I couldn't stop thinking about you. I hoped it would be better when you'd gone, but every day has been worse than the last one. I keep looking for you, listening for the sound of your voice, and I've realised that it's you that I need, not a secretary. I could get a new secretary, but I couldn't get a new you.'

He risked a glance at Tess, but she was still staring at him as if she couldn't believe what she was hearing, and he ploughed on before she had a chance to laugh in his face and tell him that he was too late, that she was quite happy with Steve Robinson and her great new job.

'I know you're OK on your own,' he said. 'I've always been OK on my own, too. I guess I still would be if you don't... I'll survive, anyway.' He swallowed. 'I just wondered whether we might be OK together. I thought we might be more than OK. I thought we might be happy.'

He paused then, and his smile twisted. 'I guess this sounds crazy. I'm the boss from hell, aren't I? I don't expect you to believe me straight away, Tess. All I ask is a chance to make up for all the times I've shouted at you or snapped at you or made your life difficult. I thought if maybe we could go out, we could start again,' he said, sounding less sure of himself than Tess had ever heard him.

He tugged at the knot of his tie as if it felt too tight, and took a breath. 'I guess I'm just trying to ask if you would like to go out to dinner.'

It was so little to ask that Tess almost laughed. She couldn't believe that this strong, successful man should be stumbling awkwardly over his words, that he could be so blind. Didn't he know how much she loved him? Couldn't he *see*?

'Dinner?' she repeated, a smile trembling on her lips. 'Now?'

'Yes.'

'You mean like on a date?'

He set his jaw. 'Yes.'

She could feel warmth spilling through her like sunshine. 'Where were you thinking of? Cupiditas?'

'Wherever you like.'

Tess pretended to consider it, then shook her head. 'I'm not really hungry,' she said.

'We don't have to eat.' An edge of desperation crept into Gabriel's voice. 'We could go to a bar, to a movie. We could do anything you want.'

'I don't want to go out,' she said, and he stared at her for a moment before his shoulders slumped.

'Sure, I understand,' he said flatly. He shifted forward in the armchair, making ready to stand up. 'Thanks for listening, anyway. I just had to tell you how I felt, but I'll get out of your way now.'

He looked so defeated that Tess was sorry she'd teased him. 'Don't go,' she said softly as she got to her feet and went over to him.

He stared blankly up at her as she bent to lift his hands out of the way. Slack with surprise, he let her push them aside as she sat down on his lap and put her arms around his neck.

'I don't want to go out with you,' she whispered against his mouth. 'I want to stay in.'

'Tess,' he mumbled incredulously as she kissed him. 'Tess...' Recovering from the shock, his arms encircled her while his lips moved wonderingly against hers. 'Tess, what are you saying?'

'I love you,' she told him, kissing his cheek, his jaw, his mouth once more. 'I love you,' she said between kisses. 'I love you. I need you. I've missed you, too.'

Suddenly afraid that he was dreaming, Gabriel twined his fingers in her wet hair and held her head still so that he could look deep into her starry eyes.

'Say that again,' he said urgently.

'I love you.'

'But you can't love me. I'm grouchy and crabby and selfish... I've never done anything to make you love me.'

Tess smiled lovingly at him. 'There's no accounting for it,' she teased him, 'but there it is. I do. I think I've loved you since the day Harry arrived and we changed his nappy together.'

Almost giddy with relief, Gabriel began to laugh. 'I've got more romantic memories than that,' he said. 'Like waking up with you the next morning...do you remember that?'

'I remember,' whispered Tess, winding her arms more tightly round his neck so that their mouths could meet in a long, sweet kiss. 'I didn't want you to stop,' she confessed with a blissful sigh.

Gabriel smiled wickedly against her throat. 'Next time I won't.'

'Is that a promise?' she murmured, her lips moving provocatively along his jaw.

'It's a promise,' he said, his voice ragged with desire, and his arms tightened around her, enfolding her, loving her, his hands moving possessively over her as they kissed, and kissed, and kissed again.

It was some time before Tess could speak. Breathless with happiness, she laid her head on Gabriel's shoulder and snuggled into him, resting her face against his throat. 'I wish I'd known.' She sighed contentedly, thinking of the long, miserable nights she had spent trying not to cry. 'Why didn't you tell me you loved me?'

'I didn't know myself until that evening you came round to cook the romantic meal. It felt so right to kiss you then, I couldn't believe that you didn't feel anything, but on the Monday you were so unapproachable that I thought you must be regretting it. And then when you told me you were leaving…' he grimaced at the memory '…it seemed as if you just wanted to forget the whole thing.'

'I was just terrified that you would guess how much I loved you,' said Tess.

Gabriel smoothed the hair away from her face as he kissed her once more. 'Then why didn't you stay that night?'

'I was a coward, like you said but, if it's any comfort, I regretted it all the way home.'

'I wish you'd come back.'

'I did.'

He lifted his head in surprise. 'You did?'

'I saw Fionnula going into your apartment, and decided she must be on her way up to see you.'

'She was.' Gabriel told her how he had rushed to let Fionnula in. 'I thought it was you,' he remembered. 'When I saw her, I realised just how much I'd wanted you to come back. I knew then that making love wouldn't be enough, after all. I wanted you to love me the way I loved you.'

Tess sat up so that she could look into his eyes. 'I do,' she said, and kissed him softly.

'All that time we've wasted,' Gabriel pretended to grumble, when they could speak again.

'We won't waste any more,' she consoled him. 'We've got the rest of our lives together.'

'Is that a promise?' he said, taking her face between his hands.

'It's a promise,' she said.

'How long do these promises of yours last?' Gabriel asked, and Tess smiled as she kissed him again.

'A promise is for ever.'

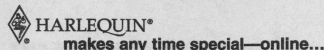

HARLEQUIN®
makes any time special—online...

shop eHarlequin

♥ Find all the new Harlequin releases at everyday great discounts.

♥ Try before you buy! Read an excerpt from the latest Harlequin novels.

♥ Write an online review and share your thoughts with others.

reading room

♥ Read our Internet exclusive daily and weekly online serials, or vote in our interactive novel.

♥ Talk to other readers about your favorite novels in our Reading Groups.

♥ Take our Choose-a-Book quiz to find the series that matches you!

authors' alcove

♥ Find out interesting tidbits and details about your favorite authors' lives, interests and writing habits.

♥ Ever dreamed of being an author? Enter our Writing Round Robin. The Winning Chapter will be published online! Or review our writing guidelines for submitting your novel.

If you enjoyed what you just read,
then we've got an offer you can't resist!

Take 2 bestselling love stories FREE!

Plus get a FREE surprise gift!

WHITE WEDDINGS

Their Big Day... and first night!

The church is booked, the flowers are arranged, the dress is ready.... But the blushing bride and groom haven't yet stepped beyond the bedroom door!

Find out why very modern brides still wear white on their Big Day, in our brand-new miniseries in

Harlequin Romance®

starting with:

REBECCA WINTERS:
The Bridegroom's Vow
(March 2002, #3693)

BETTY NEELS:
Emma's Wedding
(May 2002, #3699)

And you're invited to two more wonderful white weddings later in 2002 from award-winning authors

LUCY GORDON and RENEE ROSZEL

HARLEQUIN®
Makes any time special®